THE NEW RECRUIT

ELISE ABRAM

EMSA
PUBLISHING

PUBLISHED BY EMSA PUBLISHING
http://emsapublishing.com

The New Recruit is printed in Century Schoolbook.

Credits: Cover fonts: Gabriele Ribbon FG by Andreas Höfeld. Cover art: " Afraid teen girl in hood" ID 42764967 © Dontcut | Dreamstime.com; "Explosion" by WillZukPhotos | Flickr.com under CC 2.0 licence; Newspaper by Sandid | Pixabay.com under CCO Public Domain licence.

ALSO BY ELISE ABRAM

CHAPTER ONE

If I had to pick a moment, that single, deciding moment when everything went south, it would have to have been when my father told me he'd lost his job.

Dad had a job at a food distribution plant, picking and shipping customer orders. Kind of middle management. It paid good, but it didn't pay well. We'd been comfortable since Mom had died because they'd had this insurance policy that paid off the mortgage in the case of one of their deaths. Dad said he had connections, that one of the suppliers he knew wanted to hire him, but that didn't pan out. The world, it seemed, was in a recession. Businesses were failing everywhere. Stores were closing down all over the place, which meant that even the suppliers who had wanted to steal him away from his boss when he had one could no longer afford to hire him.

After a few weeks, Dad got a retail job making barely more than minimum. Though his biggest expense was his car, we needed it to get around, and so we had to find other ways to tighten our belts. Dad swore he'd do his best to make sure our lifestyle wouldn't change, and though he'd never admit it, it was a promise he couldn't keep.

The first major change came when I couldn't make my tuition the following semester. Mom and

Dad were big proponents of parochial Jewish school. They'd both been raised in the public system. They'd grown up celebrating the major religious holidays— Rosh Hashanah (the Jewish New Year), Yom Kippur (the Day of Atonement), Passover, and (more fun than religious) Chanukah—and both had done a stint at after school Hebrew school, but none of them was particularly Jewish. Because they'd felt unprepared to teach me themselves, they'd decided, long before I was born, to send me to parochial school so I'd know what it meant to be Jewish.

I hated it. Dad and I enjoyed pork roast, ribs, and cheeseburgers at home, and celebrated birthdays at Mandarin (all you can eat Chinese), a fact I had to hide from my friends and classmates. I had to wear this ugly uniform at school—a skirt that went practically to my ankles, and my elbows had to be covered, even when the weather was thirty-plus degrees outside. I hated it, but I knew how much it mattered to them and so I didn't complain. Maybe if I'd known how much it cost, I might have persuaded them to let me go public sooner.

Dad had a meeting with my principal and they offered to subsidize my tuition. When Dad said he still couldn't afford it, the principal suggested he take out a mortgage on his house. But when I caught my noble father sitting at the kitchen table one night, crunching numbers with his calculator, actually considering the consequences of a mortgage, I put my foot down. He looked up at me (I swear I saw tears in his eyes) and smiled, though whether out of relief or pride, I couldn't tell.

When second semester began, I was registered at the local high school. My first day was scary. I was alone. I'd known the girls at Jewish school since I was in kindergarten, but there?

My dad had wanted to walk me in, but I decided that was uncool—I didn't want to start my first day as the Daddy's Girl—and decided to go it alone. I stepped into the foyer of the school and it felt like stepping into a shopping mall, with its vaulted ceiling and green glass skylights. There were trees, actual trees, growing up from grates in the tiled floor. Further down the hall were banks of lockers. Much to my surprise, there was no dress code—boys and girls wore pants, skinny jeans, or baggy sweats. No one wore kippas, but quite a few girls wore hijabs. My school, my previous school, had been populated by a homogeneous lot, and because of the uniforms, everyone had dressed the same, with the boys wearing pants and kippas, and the girls wearing skirts and sleeves.

This was definitely going to take some getting used to.

I looked down at my own clothes, an A-line, mid-calf skirt and baggy sweatshirt; I definitely needed to rethink my wardrobe.

"You look lost," a girl said to me.

I looked up and forced a smile. "I'm new."

She smiled back. Her hair was dyed ombre, something we weren't allowed to do at my old school. "Do you have a locker?"

I shook my head.

"A schedule?"

Another head shake.

"You should probably start at the office. Do you know where that is?"

I shook my head again.

She smiled, something warm and friendly; I'd have to find her again later and see if we could be friends. "Come with me." We turned right and walked down a narrow corridor. "I'm Jem, by the way. My mom loved that cartoon growing up." I must've looked at her weird sideways because she said, "*Jem and the Holograms*?" She gasped. "Oh! You should totally come over and see that movie with me some time. My dad? He's like this techno-geek? He has the entire basement wired like a movie theatre. I have the movie on Blu-ray." She paused. "Okay, so my *mom* has the movie on Blu-ray, but she'll let us watch it if we want."

I was thrilled. Here I was, not ten minutes into my public high school career, and I already had a friend and future plans. Okay, so they weren't exactly firmed-up plans, but I was ready to take whatever I could get. The mom thing freaked me out a bit. Moms were hard to swallow, seeing as I didn't have one anymore, and being around them only made me want mine even more. I decided that Jem's mom would be the type to stay in the shadows, calling down to see if we wanted snacks and then making Jem go up to get them, rather than coming down into the basement to serve us herself.

"I didn't catch your name," Jem said.

"Judith," I told her.

"Nice to meet you, Judy."

"Not Judy; Judith. Judy reminds me of that Jewish kids' singing duo, Judy and David."

Jem's look grew stern. "You got something against Jews, Judith?"

I felt my eyes grow wide with surprise, A: that she'd straight up ask something like that, and B: as if me and my parochial school style clothes didn't tip her off that I was a Jew. "No," I said. I let out a short, snorty guffaw. "God, no. It's just that my cousin was addicted to them when she was young, and I've listened to enough of their music to last several lifetimes."

"I myself have a younger sister who still worships Judy and David," she said, kind of formal-toned. "So, good answer." She opened the office door for me and said, "You may pass."

Okay—so my new friend was kind of weird, but she seemed like fun, too. She took good care of

8

me, introducing me to the office secretary who issued me a locker and then sent us to Guidance where I got my schedule.

We compared notes and discovered we had a common lunch and the same period three English class. We made arrangements to meet for lunch, and Jem walked me to my first class.

The rest of the first day went smoothly, I guess. All classes were kind of awkward, seeing as I knew no one, spoke to no one, and no one spoke to me. Jem introduced me to her friends at lunch and in period three English, and I recognized a few girls from my earlier classes. I left school feeling kind of good about the day. I had even higher hopes that the next day would exceed that day's experiences.

Dad was still at work when I got home, but he'd left a meatloaf in the fridge with instructions for me to put it into the oven. Dad is like the Ground Meat King. He can do a million and two dishes with it, everything from chili to shepherd's pie, to this awesome dish he calls "deconstructed cabbage rolls". His meatloaf rocks. He has about ten different ways to make it, and he's adding to his repertoire all the time. That night he'd prepared what he calls his Sweet-and-Sour Meatloaf. He makes it with this sauce of molasses and soy and enough garlic to drop a vampire at fifty feet. I love the way it smells when it cooks, knowing that it will taste even better.

With dinner in the oven, I decided to check out my wardrobe. I pulled everything from my closet and drawers and divided everything into three piles like they do on those hoarding shows on television: keep, trash, and donate. I don't own a lot of clothes, seeing as I had to wear an ugly uniform most of the time, so it didn't take long, but at the end of it, my trash pile held a few single socks and some holey underwear; my donate pile had everything from my uniforms to the skirt I'd worn that day; and my keep pile was made up of exactly three pairs of jeans, one pair of leggings, two sweats, a few sweatshirts and sweaters, and some t-shirts. Depression sunk in. I needed clothes—badly—but didn't have the money to buy any. I had about five hundred dollars in my savings account, the aggregate sum of almost a decade of birthday and Chanukah gifts, but Dad insisted I save that for post-secondary school. I could ask Dad, and knowing he didn't like to say no to his little girl, I'm sure he'd oblige with the cash, but I didn't want to take advantage.

I decided I needed to get a job, so the next day after school, I made a bee-line for the mall. Lots of places were asking for extra help, but they all wanted me to apply online, so I went home and filled out as many digital applications as I could find.

I didn't hold out much hope, as my only experience was volunteering at school during their Chanukah toy drive, or at the local food bank over the summer, but I got a call from a clothing store the next day. The manager conducted a phone interview with me and asked me to come in the very next day for a face-to-face interview.

We met in the Food Court at the mall and talked for almost half-an-hour about my volunteer and school experience, as well as why I wanted to work at their store. "My mom died a few years back," I said, garnering her sympathy. "It's just been my dad and me ever since, and Dad got laid off a few months ago," I said.

The manager's face went blank, as if I'd caught her even further off guard than when I'd played the Dead Mom Card, and she had no idea how to react, let alone what to say.

"I need this job to help out, to try to make ends meet." I hoped I sounded responsible and sincere. Not wanting to destroy any credibility I might have built with the manager thus far, I decided not to add that working in a clothing store would also help me build my much-needed wardrobe, now that I no longer had to wear that gross-looking uniform, and given the 30% discount they offered their employees.

We talked a bit more and then ended the interview with, "We'll be in touch," before she said goodbye.

I sat at the table, playing the interview over in my head—what I'd said, what I shouldn't have said, what I didn't say but should have...

After the self-debrief, I decided I'd done quite well and deserved a reward, so I went to Tim Hortons, bought an Oreo Ice Capp and a Red Velvet Cookie, and took another seat.

That's when *he* approached me. "This seat taken?" he asked.

Thinking he meant he wanted to take the spare chair at the table to use elsewhere, I said, "No," but much to my surprise, he sat down across from me instead.

He took a sip from the coffee cup he'd been carrying. "Looking for a job?" he asked. His eyes were a striking turquoise, the colour you need to wear contacts to achieve.

"How did—"

"I saw your interview."

"Oh," I said. I took a careful sip of my Ice Capp, letting it melt in my mouth before swallowing to stave off brain freeze.

"How did it go?"

"Okay, I guess."

"Not much of a talker, are you?"

"You mean the interview?"

"I mean now."

"Oh." Dad always said I'd have the guys flirting with me any day now. I wondered if this was the day.

"My card," he said. He handed me a business card, which I thought was weird. I mean, how many teenage guys carried business cards with them? Unless he was older than he looked, like those actors who played teenagers long into their twenties.

I read the card. "Cain Barrett. Recruiting." I looked up into those blue-green eyes and felt I was drowning. "Who do you recruit?"

"People." I took offense to his evasiveness. He was the stranger approaching me—shouldn't *I* be the evasive one?

"Like who? For what?"

"For...things," he said matter-of-factly, as if I should already know.

I laughed, probably out of discomfort rather than amusement. What was on his agenda? Was his aim to flirt? Pick me up? Hire me for a job? Something more sinister?

"Things?" I asked.

"I work for a non-profit. We mostly raise money for the less fortunate—you know: selling flowers, silent auctions, organizing craft shows, stuff like that." He smiled and my creep-dar went up a notch.

"You were watching me?" I asked, remembering what had led to the conversation. He'd said he'd seen my interview, but he didn't approach me until *after* I'd bought my Ice Capp. That meant he'd been following me. And while the remote possibility that he'd just happened to be in the Food Court sitting near us, happened to be near enough to overhear our conversation, and then happened to see me again after I'd bought my drink was possible, I don't believe in coincidence.

"Well, when you put it that way—"

"Well, how would *you* put it?" Besides stalking, I mean.

He chuckled nervously and smiled, and I remembered why I was still talking to him. He was cute. It had to be the dimples. And the spiky hair. And the eyes, definitely the eyes. "I saw a damsel in distress and thought I'd help out. You know, be your knight in shining armor."

"And how do you propose to do that, Sir Cain?" Did that score too high on the flirtation scale? Did I mention I used to go to a religious school where the boys and girls were separated and like oil and vinegar, couldn't ever mix?

"Why, by coming to your rescue, Princess...?"

He made it sound like a question, so I said, "Judith."

"At your service, Princess Judith."

I remembered what he'd said before I'd introduced myself, and I cocked my head and squinched my eyebrows together. "Rescue? Why, whatever do you mean, squire?"

He chuckled again. It was an amazing sound, the sound of Cain's laugh. Equally amazing was the mellowing effect it had on me, making me believe he and I could be friends. More than friends, if we chose. "Keep the card. Think about my non-profit, about me. Call me if you're interested." Then he did this amazing thing: he took a step back and bowed with a flourish. "Later, my fair lady."

"Wasn't there a movie with that name?"

"Would you prefer Dame Judith?"

"Isn't that taken, too?"

He looked at me, grinned, and winked. I liked this banter and the giddiness I felt. My first flirtation. Judging by his reaction, I seemed to be doing okay with it. "I think that's Dame *Edna*," he said. "You know, that cross-dresser with the purple hair?"

"I was thinking more along the lines of Dame Judy Dench."

He smiled again, brought his palm to his mouth, made a kissing noise, and blew the kiss to me. "Till we meet again," he said.

I watched as he walked away, the words, "Count on it," sticking in my throat.

CHAPTER TWO

I told Jem about my encounter with Cain and showed her his card at lunch the next day. We were sitting on the floor in front of our lockers, trying to keep our voices down so the teacher in the room nearby wouldn't poke her head out of the door and tell us to use our inside voices or we'd have to move. She was trying to administer a test or get some work done or take a nap or something.

"So?" Jem asked.

"So what?" I said.

"Didja call him?"

I let out a guffaw. "No."

"Why not?"

I shrugged.

She turned the card over in her hand and said, "What's he recruit?"

I shrugged again. "He said he could get me a job."

"Is he cute?"

"*So* cute!"

"Tell me."

I felt myself smile. "He had this whole spiky hair thing going on, gorgeous green eyes, and dimples—"

"He did *not* have dimples."

"Oh...he had dimples. And his smile..."

"Call him!"

"I don't know."

"I do!" she said, loudly. I shushed her; better me than the teacher. "Call him."

"I don't know. I mean, I have, like, this whole *Breaking Amish* thing about me, you know? Like I've been sequestered by my religion for so long that I don't know how to react in the real world."

"You were only religious at school. Your home life was perfectly normal, so stop feeling sorry for yourself."

"That's not what I meant. I never got together with my school friends after hours. As far as I know, a boy's never even looked at me, and now this guy just approaches me in the mall, of all places?"

"He obviously likes you—"

"He listened to my interview and followed me to Tim's. I don't know whether to be flattered or creeped out."

"Call him."

I hesitated, but said, "I will."

Jem picked my phone up from the floor and handed it to me. "Call him!" she said, loudly enough for me to need to shush her again.

"I will," I repeated, "just...not now, not in school. I don't want him to hate me because I got him into trouble at his school."

Dad worked late that night; it was the perfect opportunity to call Cain. Even though I was home alone, I went into my room, got into bed, and cocooned myself in my blankets to make the call.

It rang four times before Cain answered. His voice sounded like silky syrup. He made the word "Hello" sound more beautiful than "How do I love thee?" It was so beautiful, in fact, I thought about how my twangy voice that sounded so weird on a recording (and therefore on the phone, I surmised) could ever compare, and I froze.

"Hello?" he said again. "Judith?" How could he possibly know I was the caller? "Is that you?"

Call display. Of course. My utter mortification factor kicked itself up a notch. I had no choice but to answer. "Hi, Cain."

"I'm glad you called."

That was hard to believe. A boy was glad *I'd* called him. "You are?"

"Of course I am."

I couldn't believe it. Someone like Cain was glad *I'd* called him? I half expected him to hang up when he'd learned it was me. "Um...how are you?"

"I'm good. Especially now." He sounded so confident. How did he do that? "How are you?"

"Uh...fine?"

"Are you sure?" He laughed. It sounded like a soft drumroll.

"I'm..." Falling apart. Turning to mush. Light headed. "Fine."

"To what do I owe this honour?"

"I...what?"

He laughed again and I melted further under my blankets. "Why did you call?"

"I...uh..." My heart started to beat double-time, and I found it hard to breathe.

"I'm sorry," I said. "I can't," and as if it had a mind of its own, my hand pulled my phone from my ear and hit the End Call button.

Stupid, my inner voice said. So stupid. The one time a boy shows any sort of interest and you bail. Typical.

Ordinarily, I would tell the voice to shut up, but not that time. That time I deserved it.

Air head. That's what he thinks of you.

The tears began to flow.

The next time he sees you in the mall he'll probably run in the other direction. Stupid, stupid girl.

Just then my phone buzzed twice, followed by the ding of two bells. I looked at the phone. A banner ran across the top of the monitor that read, "Text Message from Cain Barrett."

Damn call display.

I unlocked my phone and opened the text message.

u ok it said.

The phone buzzed and dinged again as I read.
u still there

here, I answered.

can I call u

I thought about it for a moment and then typed, *no. severe social anxiety at awkward situations.* I wanted to somehow convey that, as cliché as it sounded, it was me and not him, but I still wanted him to know that I sorta kinda liked him and wanted to continue the conversation, so I followed the text with a happy face emoji.

can we text instead I asked.

yes

What do I say now? What should I ask next?
where u go to school

don't. graduated.

how old r u anyway

19

Three years older than me. Three years was nothing. Dad was six years older than Mom and they seemed to get on okay. We learned in Health that boys mature slower than girls. The way I figured, I was at least at old as him mentally, maybe older.

u? he asked.

16

sweet 16

There was a long pause as I tried to figure out where to go from there. Every fibre of my being told me to end the conversation and block his number, but there was something exciting about talking to an older mystery man like that, and I couldn't help myself—I wanted more.

where u go to school

I told him.

when u finish I asked.

last year, he said.

no post secondary

didn't need it. jojo recruited me straight after.

There was that word again: recruited. I wondered what it meant. Instead I asked, *jojo?*

sort of my boss.

I saw my chance. *what u do*

sort of jack of all trades

whatever jojo needs

That didn't really help. *give me a for instance*

find out for urself

What did that mean?

bunch of us selling daffodils for cancer on weekend

join us

6 hrs of fun and community service

how can u go wrong?

When I didn't answer, he texted, *u need volunteer hrs?*

Volunteer hours were the bane of every high schooler's existence. It was something instituted by the government—forty documented volunteer hours before graduation. Though it was meant to teach humility to youth and draw the community together, it was incredibly daunting to find the time to fill the requirements, given the amount of homework heaped on us. Not to mention the fact that my father was drowning in debt and I'd much rather be working for money than for free.

Then again, it was Cain asking, he who rocked his dimples.

some, I texted.

6 hours plus hot chocolate and pizza

say yes

I thought for a moment before replying.

where and when

meet me at r table in the food court saturday morning at 9

Our table. We had a table. Me and Cain.

kk

1 thing pj

pj?

princess judith

?

its ok to say ur volunteering but dont say its with me

why not

id rather stay in the shadows

the man behind the machine

kk, I said. cu

its a date, he replied.

A date. With Cain.

PJ. Princess Judith. His pet name for me.

I kind of liked that.

CHAPTER THREE

C ain was waiting for me in the Food Court when I arrived, sitting at a two-seater table, two cups in front of him. He stood when he saw me, waited for me to get close enough, and then pulled me into an embrace. His cologne had just the right mix of spice and acridity. He looked as if he hadn't shaved in a few days, and the shadow on his cheeks suited him.

"I got you this," he said, handing me one of the cups on the table.

I thanked him and took a sip. Half dark roast coffee, half hot chocolate. Kind of creepy that he knew, especially since I'd bought an Ice Capp on the day we'd met. And here I'd thought it was weird he'd known I was interviewing for a job on the day we'd met. The fact he knew I liked the bittersweet combo of dark roast coffee and hot chocolate was downright uncanny. "How did—"

"I just got two of what I wanted." His face dropped and he looked as if he realized he'd put his foot into his mouth. "Is it too sweet? I can get you a coffee if you'd prefer."

So not stalky, as it turned out. Just a lucky guess. "It's fine. It's what I usually order." I took another sip to prove I was satisfied with the drink.

"Where are the others?" I said once I'd swallowed.

"Loading up. They said they'd text when they were here. I thought we could talk in the meantime."

Talk. It was kind of a disaster when we'd tried it over the phone. Maybe face to face would be better. Then again, maybe staring at each other with nothing to say would only serve to amplify the awkwardness instead. "I'd like that," I said, and I did, sort of, so it wasn't a total lie.

He took a sip of his drink, probably to hide his embarrassment at the situation. It was the classic tale: boy meets girl, boy likes girl, boy and girl realize they have nothing in common and drift apart. Jem would say my story was cynical. I'd call it expected. It was the first time I was sort of alone with a boy, ever. Talking to boys like they were ordinary people required a knack which I had yet to acquire.

"So," he said, breaking the awkward silence.

I smiled at the realization that he probably felt as awkward as I did. "So," I said.

"How's school?"

Weird.

Maybe not so much when you consider that was the first thing I chose to ask him about on the phone the other day. "Good," I said.

"What's your favourite subject?"

I thought for a moment, almost blurting "lunch," which was an inside joke I had with my dad. "English, I guess."

"Why English?"

"I like reading. And writing. I want to take Writer's Craft in grade twelve."

"And then you can write the next Great Canadian Novel and I can say, 'I knew her when.'"

I felt my cheeks grow hot and red. "As if!"

"It could happen. I have faith in you, Judith."

"What about you?" I asked. "What is—what *was*—your favourite subject when you were in school?"

"You're going to laugh." He took another sip of his drink and so did I.

"I swear I won't."

"Really?"

"Scout's honour."

"Okay, I'm going to ignore the fact that you're a girl and you were probably never a Scout."

I meant to take a small, silent sip of my mocha, but it wound up being more like a slurp. "Fun fact? The Scouts of Canada have been co-ed for almost a decade now."

"And you know that how?"

"My dad was a Scout. Loved it when he was a kid. There were no Girl Guide troops in our area so he inquired about the Scouts."

"And did you go?"

"No," I shook my head. "I hated to disappoint him, but Scouts was *his* dream. I wanted gymnastics lessons instead."

"You're a gymnast?"

"Turns out I wasn't any good at it and so I quit a few years in."

"I'm sorry to hear that." His lips curled into a wicked sort of grin. "I bet you were really cute in your bodysuit and tutu and hair tied up in pigtails."

"This is a fantasy you have about me?"

"It wasn't until you said you used to take gymnastics."

I took another sip and while I drank, it dawned on me he hadn't answered my question, so I asked it again.

"Civics," he said.

"You have *got* to be kidding." Along with the volunteer hours, a mandated, half-semester Civics course, as well as a mandated, half-semester Careers course, were the bane of every high schooler's existence. Politics is not my strong suit, rendering Civics the most useless, boring course I ever took in my life.

I told this to Cain and he said, "Civics is the backbone of society. Without politics and citizenship, society would be lost."

"Well, when you put it that way..."

Cain's phone vibrated and made a noise that sounded like Tinkerbell. He picked it up and read the notification. "Hail, hail, the gang's all here," he said. "Let's go." He stood, waited for me to stand, and led me toward the mall exit, his hand burning as it made contact with the small of my back.

Cain introduced me to the others in his group and they put me to work right away. I spent the next six hours selling plastic daffodil pins from a tray suspended by a ribbon around my neck, like those old-fashioned cigarette girls you see in movies. Cain disappeared shortly after getting me set up.

We broke for a half-hour lunch break, during which they served us subs. I looked everywhere, but Cain was nowhere to be found. I asked a few of the kids if they'd seen him, and though every guy I questioned thought Cain was cool, and every girl seemed to think he was McDreamy or McSteamy or some other McName, no one knew where he was. The closest I came to locating him was when one of the guys told me he was probably with Jo-Jo in an offhanded way. It was like there were only two places for Cain to be: here or with Jo-Jo.

It wasn't much to go on, but I started to wonder who this Jo-Jo character was, if it was a boy or a girl, and why Cain preferred his or her company to mine.

When they brought us coffees around two pm, I started to question why I was still there. I mean, when Cain had invited me to volunteer, he'd made it sound as if he'd be right there volunteering alongside me. And while he never came right out and said it, why would he invite me only to dump me shortly thereafter?

I felt like I did that time Dad had practically forced me to go to a B'nai B'rith youth meeting because he was convinced I needed to make new friends. Everyone was friendly at first, but the longer I hung around, the more often I went, the harder it seemed I had to work to fit in, until it was no longer worth the effort. My fellow volunteers, who were quite friendly when Cain had first introduced me, had broken into cliques over lunch and had left me to my own devices by coffee time.

I was just about ready to pack it in when Cain rematerialized. He emerged from the sliding door of an unmarked, white van and waved us toward him. "Quittin' time," he said with a grin. A few of the girls beside me giggled.

"Bring it in," he said.

The boy standing beside me said, "Let's go," and nudged me toward the van with his elbow.

"Hey," Cain said with a wink when I met him at the van. He was squatting inside, surrounded by white, cardboard trays, each of them with a yellow ribbon tied from one side to the other, and I got the feeling this wasn't his only stop. I started wondering if he hadn't abandoned me because he was busy coordinating volunteers at several locations, and his behaviour suddenly made sense.

Cain took the tray from me, his hand lingering on mine as he brushed against it, sending the good kind of shivers through my body. "Missed you," he said.

Embarrassed when my cheeks flushed, I looked down at the pavement to bury my smile.

When he had collected all of the trays, Cain said, "Okay everyone. Pile in." He pointed out a few kids, saying "you" with each one. "Michael will be here soon. The others can ride with him.

"Judith, you're up front with me."

I thought I heard tongues cluck and an "aww" or two from the girls in the back of the truck, disappointed that Cain had insisted I was the one to ride shotgun with him.

"Where are we?" I asked. Cain had turned into the dirt driveway of a one storey bungalow. The roof was missing a few shingles and the shutters needed a good paint job. It looked out of place, given its run-down appearance in the middle of the city, and the fact that it sat in the centre of an otherwise empty lot. Tall grass grew in the front and back yards, though it had been flattened by a number of beat up cars and pick-up trucks in the side yard.

"Jo-Jo's," Cain said.

"Who's that?"

The girls in the back giggled. Whoever Jo-Jo was, it appeared I was the only one who had yet to have the pleasure of his acquaintance. I looked back at them, feeling my eyebrows knit closer together.

"Jo-Jo? He's like...like our Scoutmaster. "

Until that moment, I'd assumed the kids selling flowers with me were a bunch of rag-tag volunteers. I had no idea they were that organized.

Cain put the car into park and opened the door. I had a choice at that point, to go with Cain into Jo-Jo's den, or run in the other direction and try to find my way home. I've always suffered a sort of social anxiety in new situations. To go into a stranger's house with a group of strangers for any length of time seemed like the scariest thing I could ever think of at that (or any other) particular moment in time.

My car door opened, startling me out of my fear-induced paralysis.

"Coming?" Cain asked, holding the door with one hand and his other hand out to me.

I looked up into his green-blue eyes made watery by the wind, and took his hand. Yes, it would be scary as all get-out walking over that threshold, even holding Cain's hand, and yes, I would be surrounded by strangers, but it would be with Cain at my side.

Cain took my hand and I let him pull me out of the car, where I found myself standing nose to nose with him. We looked into each other's eyes for a moment and my heart fairly stopped as I pondered how awkward it felt. Then I thought about how it might feel to have him kiss me before we parted. Then I thought about what he might think if *I* kissed *him* before we parted instead.

Cain smiled and took a step back. Still holding my hand he led me toward Jo-Jo's place, closing the car door on the way.

A tall, barrel-chested man older than my father greeted us at the door. He hugged Cain, who let go of my hand long enough to hug the man back.

"And who have we here?" the man said in a baritone growl.

"This is Judith," Cain said, guiding me toward the man. "Judith, meet Jo-Jo."

I held my hand out for him to shake. He said, "We don't stand on formality here, Judith," and he pulled me into a near suffocating bear hug, which was weird and kind of scary, seeing as we'd only just met.

Cue the social anxiety.

I took a deep breath, but got a lungful of Jo-Jo's cologne instead of fresh air, and coughed.

"Careful, Joj," Cain said. "You'll smother her!"

Jo-Jo let go. I felt Cain's hand snake into mine and pull me closer.

"It's okay, Judith. We're like one big, happy family here. You'll see.

"Make yourselves at home. Cain, show her around. Introduce her to some of the kids. Dinner should be here any minute now."

I looked over my shoulder at Cain. "It's okay. Jo-Jo's like the papa bear around here." Cain unzipped his jacket and hung it up in the front closet, and I did the same. When I looked back at him, I noticed he was wearing a *chai*, the Hebrew letters *chet* and *yud*, forming the Hebrew word for life. Up until that moment, I hadn't known he was Jewish. As silly as it sounds, I felt a bit more relaxed. I remembered my conversation with Jem about how little I knew about him. Now I knew one more thing. My social anxiety turned itself down a notch. With this knowledge, Jo-Jo's place seemed a bit more *hamish*, a bit more like home.

Cain introduced me to a few people. Everyone seemed really nice, especially the guys. It was flattering, but uncomfortable.

We hadn't been there more than about fifteen minutes before the pizza arrived. I was playing Jewish Geography with one of the guys Cain had introduced me to, trying to figure out if, since we both had family originating in Kensington Market in the early and mid-1900s, we knew any people in common, when Cain suddenly appeared beside me with two plates of pizza.

"You keep kosher?" he asked me.

We used to. Mom virtually insisted on it. Growing up we had four sets of plates, two for milk, two for meat, two sets for everyday, and two for Passover. After Mom had died, Dad tried to keep us kosher in her memory, but the more he needed to work, the more we'd ordered in. At first, we'd ordered kosher-style, exclusively beef and chicken. But the longer the hours, the less concerned he was about what he'd bought, and Chinese from the local Chinese grocery became our go-to meal That and pizza, and there's only so much General Tao chicken and cheese pizza one can eat before getting bored. Soon we'd merged the plates and thrown kosher out the window.

But that was all TMI for Cain at this point in our relationship, so I just shook my head.

"Good," he said. He held a piece of pizza up to my mouth for me to take a bite. It was a meat lover's pizza. And though I wasn't adverse to a little pepperoni and cheese every now and then, I wouldn't ever sit down to a cheeseburger and a glass of milk, which is exactly what I tasted.

I managed to choke it down and said, "Is there any cheese and veggie?" and he offered me the other plate. I smiled my thanks and took a bite of the well-done, thin crust, whole wheat, cheese pizza. The taste was divine.

"What're you drinking? Coke okay?"

I'm a Pepsi girl when I have a choice, but Coke will suffice in a pinch. I nodded that it was okay, and Cain briefly disappeared and returned with two cans of Coke, the tabs already popped, straws in place.

"To our new friendship," Cain said. We clinked cans and drank.

"What is this place, anyway?" I asked after I'd swallowed my next bite.

"You know *B'nai Brith?*"

I nodded.

"This is like our own, personal *B'nai Brith.*"

29

"What's wrong with the real *B'nai Brith*?"

"Too much conformity."

"And that's bad?"

"Why so many questions, Judith?" Cain asked.

I shrugged. "Just...curious."

Why so secretive, Cain? I wanted to ask, but decided not to. I kind of liked Cain. He seemed strong. Mature. So unlike the boys I went to school with. And then there were those dimples—don't get me started. Cain excited me in a way I'd never been before. I wanted to explore my relationship with him to see where it went. Questioning his motives at this point seemed counterproductive, like I might be working toward pushing him away instead of allowing us to grow closer.

He flashed me his dimples and his green eyes lit up. "Curiosity killed the cat," he said with a chuckle.

"Is that a threat?" I asked, trying to be flirtatious.

"That depends," he said.

"On what?"

"On whether you keep asking me questions." He leaned over and pecked me on the lips, as if to let me know he was joking. "I'm getting more pizza," he said. "Want some?" I nodded and let him, and the weird conversation we just had go.

CHAPTER FOUR

When I told Jem about the pizza party with Cain, she said, "Did you tell your father?"

"About what?"

"About Cain. About Jo-Jo."

"Okay, first? There's nothing to tell about Jo-Jo. He's like this Scoutmaster guy who organizes kids to do charity work.

"And if I tell my dad about Cain he'll just do that 'Does he celebrate Christmas or Chanukah?' shtick he does every time I mention someone new."

"Do you think he'd care if Cain wasn't Jewish?" Jem gasped. "Would he care if I wasn't Jewish?"

"I don't think he cares, it's just that old Marry Someone Of Your Own Kind mentality his parents drilled into him.

"Anyway, it doesn't matter. Cain was wearing a *chai*; he's Jewish."

"Or he was wearing it to make you *think* he's Jewish."

"Why would he do that?"

Jem shrugged. She took a sip from her coffee cup.

"You don't know Cain. He's laid back, kind, you know? Like, you look into those eyes of his and those dimples come out of hiding and—"

"Trust is more than a pretty face," Jem said, less tentatively than I would have liked. It made me mad. She didn't know Cain the way I did. I saw what he was like at the party. I saw the way he'd handled the kids selling daffodils at the mall, the way they'd listened to him as if they'd respected him. She wasn't there when we met for coffee before I volunteered, or when he'd first approached me in the mall. She didn't see the look he'd given me when we were flirting. If she had, then she'd know he couldn't be anything but sincere.

"If you're going to go around hating on Cain, we're going to have a problem."

"Chill, Jude," Jem said. While I hated "Judy" as the short form of my name, I kind of liked "Jude". Jem said it reminded her of the old Beatles song, and she often answered my phone calls with "Hey, Jude," as a result.

"Sisters before misters," she said.

"Sisters before misters," I said, and our knuckles met in a fist-bump explosion, serenaded by giggles.

My phone chimed. My giggles stopped when I saw I'd gotten a text from Cain. I felt my mouth curl into an involuntary grin.

"Who is it?" Jem asked.

"Cain," I told her.

"What's he want?"

"Privacy much?"

"You've shared everything else with me and *now* you're shy?

"He wants to get together."

"When?"

"Now. He's waiting in the parking lot outside."

Jem's eyes grew wide. "You're not going to ditch, are you?"

I raised my eyebrows and shrugged my shoulders in a kind of what-other-choice-do-I-have gesture.

"You know the computer calls home and leaves a message for absences?"

I shrugged again. "I'll delete the message."

"They email, too. Are you going to hack your dad's email to delete that, too?"

Another text from Cain: *you coming*

"I gotta go." I collected the Math homework I was supposed to be doing instead of talking about Cain and stuffed it into my locker. I stuffed my backpack and half-eaten lunch into my locker as well, grabbed my purse and my jacket, and said, "Cover for me."

Jem sat looking up at me as if she'd just lost her puppy, and so I bent down and said the only thing I could think of: "Fist bump?"

She reached up and met my fist with hers.

"You going to be okay?" I asked.

Jem smiled and nodded. "You should get going. Cain's waiting."

"Hey," Cain said when he saw me, having yet to catch onto the whole "Hey Jude" thing Jem had going on. He took a step toward me and hugged me tightly."You free?" he asked.

The five-minute warning bell beeped, and I felt its Pavlovian pull, like we'd learned in Sociology, Anthropology, Psychology class (which we not so lovingly refer to as SAP, partially because the class is an elective, and anyone who willingly signs up to take a class with the likes of Mr. Wilkins has got to be a sap). Though it was still early in the semester, I'd already been conditioned to starting and stopping classes with the bell. The need to say goodbye to Cain and run to my next class was overwhelmingly maddening. But then Cain showed me his dimples, and the regimen of my daily schedule ebbed away.

"I am, now," I told him.

He nodded and smiled again. He hadn't shaved since the last time I'd seen him and the fuzz seemed to fill out his cheeks somewhat; it looked good on him. "Then what are we waiting for?"

I went around the car and climbed in.

"I'll have you back before the end of the school day. Your father won't suspect a thing." He must have read my body language—I was looking down at my hands in my lap, debating whether or not I should tell him, and he said, "What's wrong?"

"They call home and email when we miss a class. Dad'll know."

He smiled at me again. "You have the school's number?"

"Why?"

"Watch and learn," he said.

I queued up the school's number on my phone and handed it to him. Cain dialed on his own phone.

"But won't it say your name on call display?"

"My phone comes up as caller unknown."

He held up the index finger on his free hand and said, "Yes, hello." He cleared his throat. "I'm Judith Abraham's father, and I'm calling to let you know that Judith came home for lunch with a headache, and she won't be attending classes this afternoon...yes, thank you. I'll tell her.

"All taken care of. You'll be home your normal time and no one will be the wiser."

While a part of me was in awe of Cain, a part of me grew incredibly uncomfortable. I mean, he'd just lied. To an adult. And without batting an eye. Rather than grab the door handle and run in fear, I felt a warm tingle rush through my body. What if Cain was a bad boy? Bad boys have a reputation for being exciting, don't they? I could use a bit of excitement in my hum-drum life. Plus the fact that Dad was holding down several jobs when I couldn't find even one, meant that, outside of school, I spent a lot of time alone.

"What are we waiting for?" I asked Cain. He smiled again and turned the key in the ignition.

We wound up at a local Tim Hortons, sitting in the car, drinking Ice Capps, and talking. Cain, I learned, was an only child. Both of his parents were still around, but they'd kind of washed their hands of him when he'd turned eighteen.

"That's sad," I told him.

"Why? Your dad's done the same and you're barely sixteen."

"It's not the same," I told him, feeling like I was about to cry. "Dad's doing the best he can with the deal life's given him."

"What deal? A daughter desperately in need of male affection?"

"Okay, first of all? I meant that his wife died so young. And second, who says I'm desperate?"

"You're here with me, aren't you?"

"And that makes me desperate?"

"You left school and got into a car with me and you barely know me."

What was he up to? Was he being serious? Playing Devil's advocate? My eyes burned as I fought back tears. I knew I should have turned tail and ran after the call he'd made when I'd gotten into the car.

A tear ran down my cheek. I looked up and out through the windshield. "Take me home," I said.

"Look, all I'm saying is that you were feeling neglected when you met me."

"And somehow that's a crime?"

"Not a crime. Endearing, maybe?" Up until that moment, his body had been turned toward me, but at that point, he slumped back into his seat with a huge sigh. "How did we get here, anyway?"

"You insulted my dad and then you insulted me, and now I want to go home."

"I didn't insult your dad.

"All I'm saying is that...aw, hell." He leaned forward in his seat and twisted his torso to face me again. "Judith, you're smart and beautiful and I can't believe some guy hasn't swept you up before now."

I turned to look at him, unsure whether to cry full out or smile, demand to be taken home or open the door and find my own way home. "Go on," I said.

"We're more alike than you think. Whether intentional or not, we've both been neglected by those we love. "

"My father loves me."

Cain chuckled. "I never said he didn't, just that whether or not my parents do is negotiable."

The anger I'd felt started to melt away at that statement. He was really more of a lost boy than a bad one. He felt as lonely as did I at times, and we could fix that, as long as we were together.

"It's getting close to home time. What say we start fresh and talk later?"

"No need to start fresh. I flew off the handle. I understand what you meant now," I said, and I brought a hand up to his cheek, brushing my thumb against the wiry wisp of beard he was growing. He took my hand from his cheek, brought my palm to his lips, kissed it, then lowered my hand to his heart. He smiled this huge smile and looked down and off to the side as he did, as if he were embarrassed at the show of affection.

He held his gaze and my hand for a moment, and then said, "We should get going," before letting go.

CHAPTER FIVE

Dad pulled a night shift. Jem agreed to spend the night so I wouldn't be alone. It's not that I was afraid or anything, but it sure would be a whole lot less lonely with someone there. In order for Dad to agree to a sleepover on a school night, he made the both of us swear we'd be in bed with lights out no later than eleven. Jem and I giggled when I pointed out that he'd said nothing about going to sleep.

Dad left pizza money, which we had delivered, and which we ate while binge-watching the first half of the first season of *The Walking Dead*. There's nothing like cramming your face with greasy pizza in the midst of zombies and rotting corpses. Anyway, Jem was busy fawning over how cute Carl was and insisting how Chandler Riggs was becoming a righteous hunk. When I insisted there was none of what my Dad called "eye candy" in the show for me, Jem said, "I don't blame you. Who needs fictional eye candy when you have some real eye candy of your own."

"I do *not* have real eye candy."

"What about That Cain Guy?" Cain was never just plain Cain to Jem. He was always That Cain Guy.

"What about him?"

"You said he was cute, right? All dimply, spiky-haired, and...cute."

"What do you do, record and memorize everything I say?"

Jem shrugged. "I just pay attention when you speak."

"Can we just drop Cain and watch TV, please?"

"Okay," Jem said, exaggerated, as if she were doing me a favour by not prying into my love life, not that I had one to speak of. Cain was cute, all right, what Jem would call a "righteous hunk" if she ever saw him, but I couldn't see it working out in the long run. I mean, we'd seen each other twice so far, and twice it had ended badly. Would the third time be the charm or the third strike? Would there even be a third time?

Ten minutes later my phone buzzed. I picked it up, took a quick look at my monitor, and put it back down.

"Who is it?" Jem asked.

"I don't know." The last update of my phone's operating system was stupid and it no longer showed whom my texts were from, displaying a notice that I had so many texts instead. I'd have to unlock the phone and open the app to see whom the texts were from.

My phone buzzed again.

"Another one."

"I know," I said.

"Aren't you curious?"

The text had to be one of three things: either it was Dad, or it was Cain, or it was advertising from my service provider. I had to admit: I was curious to see if it *was* Cain and if he'd sent me a Dear Judith text or a sext or something, but I didn't want to give Jem the satisfaction.

"Nope," I said, feigning interest in watching the gang try to recapture some semblance of normalcy in the zombie apocalypse and failing.

"What if it's That Cain Guy?"

"Jem," I said, taking another bite of cold pizza, "you really need to get out more."

"Check your messages, Jude."

"*You* check *your* messages."

"You know you're dying to check."

I looked up at Jem and swallowed my pizza. She was right. I *was* dying to check. "Fine," I said, feigning resignation. "You really need to get a life, you know that?"

"It's on my To-Do list. Until I get around to it, I'm just going to have to live vicariously through yours."

I unlocked my phone and opened the messages app. "It's Cain. Happy?"

Jem beamed. It was the face I imagined her making after Chandler Riggs had followed her on Twitter. "What's he say?"

I tapped his name in my list of messages and read: *Hey, you free tonight*

This is followed by: *Wanna hang*

"He wants to get together," I said, paraphrasing for her.

"When?"

"Tonight."

"Tonight would be good. No awkward excuses needed for your dad."

"I can't just leave you here."

"Why not?"

"Because you're my friend. Whatever happened to sisters before misters?"

"I would ditch you in a heartbeat if the situation were reversed."

"No, you wouldn't."

"No, I wouldn't."

I tore a piece of crust off my pizza slice, dipped it in the garlic sauce, and popped it into my mouth, chewing to buy me some time. What kind of friend would I be if I ditched Jem at my own house, alone, when the only reason she was there was to keep me company in the first place? On the other hand, if I made myself unavailable to Cain, how much longer would he hang around?

"What if my dad calls?"

"I'll run interference for you."

"How?"

"I'll tell him you're in the bathroom or something, then I'll call you and tell you to call him back."

"I could ask Cain to come here. You said you were dying to meet him."

Jem shook her head. "I'd only be a third wheel." She reached for the bag of Chicago Style popcorn. You wouldn't think cheese and caramel would mix, but the result is the crack of the comfort food world. "Text him back," she said.

Got a friend over, I texted.

"What didja say?"

Bummer, he texted back.

What about after

Sleeping over

Double bummer

"What? What?" Jem said.

"I told him no."

"Don't be stupid," she said, grabbing my phone from my hand.

I called her name and tried to get my phone back, but she practically tackled me on her way out of the room. I caught up with her on the other side of a locked bathroom door. Faint buzzes sounded out from the other side.

"Jem!" I called, banging on the door. "This is *so* not cool." I called her name again and the door unlocked. Jem came out and handed me my phone.

"What did you do?" I asked her.

"Get dressed, brush your teeth. He'll be here any minute."

"What did you do?" I asked again. I tried to unlock my phone but she'd frozen it by typing in too many incorrect passwords. "What did you tell him?"

"That you could ditch and your friend wouldn't mind."

"And?"

"That you had to be back by ten."

"What else?"

"Nothing else."

"Jem?" I asked in a warning voice.

"Nothing!" She paused for a beat and then made a noise that sounded like "ach!" and she rolled her eyes as if my behaviour were exasperating her. "I might have told him your father was out and that you were hoping he'd text because you missed him."

I tried to show her an angry face. Even if what she said was true, taking my phone and texting my maybe future boyfriend like that was crossing the line.

"Oh, tell me anything I said wasn't true."

Part of me wanted to send her home and never see her stupid face again for pulling a prank like that, but another part of me wanted to hug her for being so understanding.

"You'd better get ready. There's no turn off bigger than smelling pizza breath when he goes in for the kiss."

Cain met me in my driveway. When he saw me he got out of his car, went around to the passenger's side and opened the door for me—so romantic! He greeted me with an unexpected kiss on the cheek.

"You cool to go?" he asked once we were in the car. "I mean, it's night, and you're young, and your dad—"

Er! I wanted to shout. Young*er*! But in the interest of making this work, I said, "I'm cool. Dad's gone for the night and Jem'll cover for me if he calls."

"You sure, Jude? I don't want to make a bad impression on your dad if he finds out—"

"He won't find out." I'm good, okay? Why doesn't he get that? Why is he so set on throwing a monkey wrench into the works?

"Good, 'cause if you get grounded it only means we won't be able to see each other for a while."

Enough already! "Can we just..." Can we just drop it? Can we just stop? Can we just a million other things but talk about this! "Can we just...go?"

"Right," he said, and he turned the key in the ignition.

"Where to?" I asked as a conversation starter.

"An undisclosed, secret location," he said. And though I knew he was joking, my brain started to race. Exactly what *did* I know about This Cain Barrett Guy? He had the knack for making me feel safe, I knew that much. He made me feel wanted, made me feel pretty when we flirted. He seemed genuine in his affection for me. He was cute. He was older than me at nineteen. He'd finished high school. He had dimples. He did charity work for a living. He belonged to some youth group ran by that guy Jo-Jo which was a little like—but not as regimented as—Scouts. Listening to him speak was like listening to butter melt. He drove a car. Did I mention he was cute?

Okay, so I was reaching, but stuff like that didn't happen to me. Though my dad would disagree, I'm nothing much to look at. I'm sort of in between tall and short, between slim and what my Bubbie would say was *zaftig*. She would also say I was shaping up to be a *gut balabusta*, seeing as I was home alone all the time and had to keep house for my dad and me, and that I would make someone a good wife one day. Bubbie doesn't understand that I want to do about a million other things before I become a wife.

Make no mistake; I wasn't seeing Cain thinking we'd spend an eternity together. But even though I had Jem, life without Mom was pretty lonely. I mean, I get it: Dad needed to work to keep the roof over our heads intact, to keep clothes on my back, food in my belly, and gas in the car, but that meant I was on my own a lot, I mean, a lot. Just the thought of having someone besides Jem to keep me company, to fill my need to be taken care of instead of doing all the taking care of myself, was something that, until I'd met Cain, I could only dream about.

I nodded when he joked about our destination and said, "What are we going to do when we get there?"

"No spoilers allowed."

I was getting kind of miffed at his deflecting my attempts at meaningful conversation.

"So..." I began, feeling more and more awkward with each attempt, "where did you grow up?"

"Here and there." He took his eyes off the road briefly to flash me a smile. "My parents moved around a lot. Mostly we lived in Northern Ontario, though I think I technically went to preschool in Manitoba."

"Did you like living up north?"

Cain shrugged. "It was preschool, so I was young and don't remember much except for the snow. There's *a lot* of snow in Northern Ontario."

43

"We've always lived here. You know, the GTA. My parents always talked about how there used to be enough snow, even in the city, to build snow forts at the side of the road."

Cain chuckled. "I can count on one finger the number of times in my lifetime I've been able to do that since moving to the city." He shook his head slowly. "It's the damn government. They had the means to halt greenhouse emissions decades ago, but were too worried to affect the profit from gas sales to do anything about it."

At last! A full-on conversation. With Cain! "What confuses me is how they can say it's the greenhouse effect when there have been days, decades ago, where the temperature was the same. You know, how they say this is the hottest August sixth since 1862 or something."

Cain turned to me and smiled again. "The first rule of statistics is to throw out anomalies. You have to look for consistencies over time. One odd day of high temperatures can be the result of solar flares, or something that made too many cows flatulent on that particular day. When you look at the trend, you can't help but worry your pants off about the world a few decades from now."

I added intelligent to my mental list of what I knew about Cain; he was passionate about the environment, too.

"How do you know all this?"

"I get around."

The car fell silent again to the point of being awkward. Cain turned on the radio, presumably to fill the silence. "You like oldies?" he said.

"My dad listens to them all the time."

"Which decade?"

"Seventies and eighties mostly. He says that's when he discovered music and the songs he grew up with kind of stuck."

Cain smiled again. Tick another box off on my mental list for cute. "My parents, too. They refused to let me wear earphones in their presence. I had no choice but to run away or comply. Truth is, they kind of grow on you after a while."

My dad always lets me play my music on the car stereo through Bluetooth connection. He complains, like, a lot, but he always sings along. He probably thinks that if he butchers the lyrics of my songs enough I'll eventually stop playing them. So far his nefarious plot hasn't worked to plan.

"I guess," I tell Cain.

A hush fell between us once more, broken a moment later when the song changed on the stereo and Cain said, "Oh, I love this song."

Bohemian Rhapsody by Queen.

I remember Mom saying how much her father had loved that song every time it played. A nostalgic funk wafted around me, growing until my eyes threatened to tear. It wasn't because my zaidie, a man who died when I was only about two, liked the song, but because my mom never forgot it.

The song changed again, almost at the exact same moment Cain put his blinkers on.

"We're here," he said, and he turned onto a dark and narrow road that dead-ended with a fence and a yellow, diamond-shaped sign that read "End of Road".

CHAPTER SIX

"What is this place?" I asked Cain. We were sitting on the hood of his car, leaning back against the windshield. The dead end street had no lights and no houses on it, but one side backed onto some rather large backyards. I think it might have been an access road for the hydro field on our left.

"Lovers' Lane," Cain said, matter-of-factly.

My body tensed with regret. Why did he take me there? "Oh," I said, a little fearful of what the name implied.

"It's a pretty place, especially from this vantage. There are hardly any city lights because of the field and the backyards, and the crickets are kind of peaceful."

"Oh," I said, this time with relief. I remember reading once, that there are any number of ways to say the word "dude"—one only has to watch *Dude, Where's My Car* to figure that one out. I guess "oh" is another one of those words with infinite meaning depending on time, place, and the way it's said.

A chilly wind picked up and I shivered. "You cold?" Cain asked.

I nodded.

"There's an app for that," he said, and he hopped off the car. He came back a few seconds later with a blanket.

"What did you say?" I asked.

"It's an expression. You know, there's an app to solve every problem. My blanket is the app to solve your problem."

Proving I could be quite eloquent when I needed to, I said, "Oh," again.

Cain wrapped the blanket around both of our shoulders like a cape. His arm rested across my shoulders under the blanket, in the crook of my neck. He pulled me toward him. "This is nice," he said.

I nodded.

"I come here sometimes to be by myself. To look at the stars." He paused for a beat. "You ever do that? Gaze at the stars, wonder if there's anything out there?"

"I've tried on days there were meteor showers or eclipses, but didn't get a chance to see anything."

"Do you know the constellations?"

I looked up to the sky, searching for patterns. "I think I see the big dipper," I told him.

"Did you know there are two dippers in the sky? A big one *and* a little one?"

I shook my head. "Uh-uh."

"See the last star on the end of the dipper's cup?"

I nodded.

"Follow it across to the next brightest star. See that? That's Polaris. It's on the tip of the handle of the little dipper."

"I see it!" There was a pause while we stared at the sky. I had a million questions I wanted to ask him, about his family, his school, his work, his likes, his dislikes...When I could no longer hold my tongue I blurted, "Why are we here, Cain?"

He turned to look at me. "What do you mean?"

I sat up on the hood and said, "Do you want to make out?" and his jaw dropped. "I don't mean, let's make out, I mean...I hope you didn't bring me here to make out because I don't want to. I mean...I want to, but I'm not ready to. I mean—"

Cain's laughter stopped my case of verbal diarrhea, which was probably for the best; I'm a wreck when the social anxiety monkey rears his ugly head.

"What's so funny?" I asked him.

"You're cute when you're nervous."

"Oh," I said, back to being Articulate Judith instead of Socially Inept Judith.

"Relax, Jude. I'm not expecting anything except for us to get comfortable with each other."

There was a moment when we just looked at each other, his green eyes seemingly almost as bright as Polaris in the night sky. "I'm sorry," I said finally.

He smiled and nodded. "Nothing to be sorry about." He swiped his hand in a come here motion and welcomed me back into his embrace.

Did I actually say that I wanted to make out with him but that I wasn't ready?

For the first time since I'd left the house, I wondered about the time. Then I thought about Jem, alone in my house, doing the very thing she was supposed to be preventing me from doing. I pictured her like a vampire, waiting for me to come home so she could bleed me of any and all information I'd learned about Cain. So far that included that he liked stargazing and me.

"Want to play Two Truths and a Lie?" I asked, hoping it would help lift the mood enough for Cain to forget an awkward conversation, though it would remain branded forever into my psyche for all eternity.

"What's that?" How could he not know what that was? My teachers have been playing that with us as an ice-breaker since forever. Even if he's three or so years older than me, surely at least one teacher at one point in time had played that in one of his classes. I've even seen them play it on television once or twice.

"Don't get out much, do you?" I said to tease him.

He smiled an open-mouthed smile; his teeth almost glowed in the moonlight. "My job's sort of all-encompassing."

"So, to play Two Truths and a Lie, I tell you three things and you have to guess which is the lie. So if I say something like I'm an only child, I'm twenty years old, and I'm having a good time tonight, you have to say which one is the lie."

He chuckled. I don't know how, but he made it sound self-deprecating, and my heart leapt. "The lie...is that you're having a good time tonight."

I slapped his arm and said, "Be serious."

"Okay, okay. You're twenty years old. Challenge me, why don't you?"

"Your turn. Give me two truths and a lie."

"No, no, no. Play fair. You already told me you were sixteen. I'm serious. Give me a challenge."

"Hmmm," I said, pausing for effect. "Let me see...I'm an only child, I love *Twilight*, both the books and the movies, and...I've never had a boyfriend—"

"Until now," Cain said. He leaned over to kiss me on the lips, closed mouthed. He withdrew and went back to leaning against the windshield and looking up at the stars.

A long moment of silence passed between us as I tried to collect my thoughts. It was then I'd realized my plot had backfired. I'd brought up the game to try to learn stuff about Cain, but all that happened was that he'd learned stuff about me (the *Twilight* lie was a giveaway). How stupid was I?

I was toying with reminding him that we were in the middle of a game when he said, "You know any ghost stories?"

I shrugged. "There's the one about the guy with the hook on Lovers' Lane, but I doubt that would be scary, seeing as we're *outside* of the car."

Cain chuckled. "So right." After a breath he said, "What about the one with the hitch-hiker on the highway who leaves her sweater in the car and when the guy goes to return it—"

"The mom says her daughter died, like, ten years ago, or something."

"That's the one!"

"That might be good out here. You know, because we're on a road in the dark."

"Maybe the victim of the guy with the hook is still out here looking for a lift home." We both laughed at that one.

"Then there's the one about the minors out after curfew and the police officer."

Both of us startled at the voice which belonged to the police officer standing to my right.

"I wasn't aware of a curfew, Officer," Cain said.

"It's not safe to be out here after dark, and you're illegally parked."

"We'll leave," Cain said.

"I'm going to need to see some ID."

"Are you compelling me to show my ID?"

"I'm requesting for you to show me your identification."

"But are you *compelling* me to show it?"

I wanted to tell him I didn't mind showing the officer my ID but didn't think it wise to interrupt and risk making the situation worse.

"No, I'm not compelling you."

"Then me and my girl will pack up and leave quietly."

The policeman's posture tensed noticeably. "If I catch you here again, it will mean a fine."

"I understand." Cain pulled the blanket from the hood. The car blipped and the lights flashed when he used the fob to unlock the doors. "You have a good evening, Officer." He flashed that full-depth, winning smile at the man, threw the blanket into the backseat through the driver's door, and got into the car. I followed. The cop stood there until we'd turned and retreated down the lane toward the main street.

"That was amazing," I told Cain once we'd turned onto Bathurst Street. "How did you know to do that?"

"I just do."

"I would have been in tears without you, I mean, I don't know *what* I would have done."

"Girls—white girls, especially—hardly ever get carded. I hang with a mixed crowd, so getting carded's old hat to me. I just read up so I know my rights."

"My knight in shining armour," I said. "So brave."

It was hard to tell under the strobing streetlights in the otherwise darkened car, but I think he blushed.

I texted Jem from the driveway before I left Cain's car. He got out to walk me to the door, but I stopped him. "Jem will be waiting."

"Then we'll say our goodbyes here." He turned toward me and reached his arms around me,

51

linking his fingers at the small of my back. "I had a great time."

"Me too." We touched foreheads. "So glad it was more three on a match than three strikes."

"What?" he said. He chuckled.

"Nothing. I just...I thought it went well, too."

"Can I see you again?"

"I'd like that."

He planted a chaste kiss on my lips and my insides melted, I mean, literally melted. It felt as if my legs might turn to rubber and I'd wind up a pile of goop on the floor between his feet.

"Good night," I said, barely a whisper.

"Good night, Jude."

I took a few steps toward the front door and heard Jem click the deadbolt open.

"Oh," Cain said to get my attention. "I almost forgot: Jo-Jo might have a job for you to do, a simple package delivery. Can I pick you up after school tomorrow to discuss it?"

"If it comes with an excuse to see you again, sure." Smooth, Judith. Real smooth.

"It's a date, then."

I nodded. "It's a date."

CHAPTER SEVEN

Inside Jo-Jo's house, Cain motioned for my jacket, but I wanted to hold on to it in case I needed to make a quick getaway. Jo-Jo's house was unkempt and shady, and I don't mean there wasn't a lot of light. There were a few kids lounging in the main room. Some of them were playing Chess and it looked like they'd been at it for a while. I took a mental tally of their ages—most of them appeared to be my age, give or take a few.

I retraced my steps since I'd left the school. I'd practically ran to my locker, grabbed my jacket, and fled. Cain was already in the parking lot when I'd gotten there. The ride over there had taken 15 minutes at best. If they were my age or younger, why weren't they still in transit from their schools? If they were older, why weren't they at work?

Two girls sat on the couch opposite the television, whispering to each other and giggling.

"Take a seat," Cain said. He placed his hand on the small of my back. "I'll go let Joj know I'm here."

I nodded and perched myself on the corner of the chair. The seat was constructed from a curved piece of wood with a rectangle of pleather, held down with buttons in a diamond pattern, but the cushion didn't reach the edge of the wood, so there was a little ledge around it, kind of like a picture frame.

That's where I sat—on the corner of the frame, not on the cushion.

The girls continued to look at me and giggle. I heard one of them whisper,"I will...no, I will...shhh-shhh." They paused their colluding for a moment and then the one who said she would, said, "Home wrecker," just like that, as if we were having a normal conversation and this were a part of it.

I stayed focussed on the television. They were watching a re-run of *The Big Bang Theory*, which was about to segue into a dialogue I thought was absolutely brilliant. I was still pretty convinced they were having a private conversation at the time and the last thing I wanted to do was intrude.

"Home wrecker," the girl said, louder than before. It was then I realized they were trying to get my attention.

"I'm sorry?" I said. I'd never seen those girls before. When I arrived, I'd assumed they were regulars. If that were the case, why weren't they more welcoming?

"You heard me," she said. "You're a home wrecker," she continued, matter-of-factly, as if I should know exactly what she'd meant.

"I don't..." I turned my head so to peek into the hall down which Cain had disappeared.

"Your sweetie can't help you now," the girl said. She stood up and took a menacing step forward. Her friend grabbed her at the wrist as if to stop her, but she shook her off and continued to advance toward me.

"I should go," I said, mentally calculating if I could reach the door before the girl reached me.

It was then Cain called my name. The three of us looked toward the back hall. When Cain turned the corner, the girl's posture relaxed a bit, her head drooped, and she blushed. I took the opportunity to meet Cain at the back of the dining room, near the forked exit to the kitchen on the right and the back hallway on the left.

"Jo-Jo's ready to see you now." He put an arm around my shoulders, and I chanced a glance back at the girls when he did. The one on the couch was talking harshly to the one that had threatened me. She caught me looking and gave me the finger.

"Something wrong?" Cain asked.

"Who *are* those girls?"

"I used to go with the one on the left," he said, casually. "The other one's her friend.

"Jo-Jo's waiting."

He led me down the back hallway to what I assumed was a bedroom, the one at the end of the hall, and I stopped dead in my tracks. "What is this, like some kind of interview or something?"

"Not *like* an interview." Cain smiled. "It *is* an interview."

"In the bedroom?"

Cain laughed. It did nothing to alleviate my flight-or-fight mechanism, still in gear after the confrontation with the girls in the living room. "It's been converted to a home office."

I looked at him, trying to gauge if he was being truthful with me.

"I'd never let anything happen to you, Jude," he said. He smiled again, his blue-green eyes lighting up; my stomach did flip-flops. "Trust me," he whispered. And then he did something I'd only ever seen in movies: he brought my palm up to his lips and kissed it. I thought I might swoon.

"Are you going to be in there with me?"

"It's an interview, Jude. No chaperones allowed."

Still trying to recover from the intimacy of the last moment, I looked up at him.

"I trust Jo-Jo implicitly," he said. He must have sensed some lingering apprehension, because he said, "I'll be right outside of the door. Call me if you need me and I'll be there, okay?"

I nodded.

He opened the door at the end of the hall and I went in, a little relieved to see that the room had been set up like an office, just like Cain had said. Cain introduced us said, "Right outside the door," and then left me in the room with the man I knew only as Jo-Jo.

Jo-Jo was sitting behind his desk, the back of his chair to me. He was shuffling through some papers on a cabinet in front of him. "Sit down, please," he said. "I'll be with you in a minute."

When he turned, he looked the same as he had the previous night—grandfatherly, but in need of a shave. "Judith, right?" he said. "You were at the pizza party after the daffodils, right?"

"Yes, sir," I answered with a nod.

"Sir's a man who's been knighted," he said. "I'm Jo-Jo, please. We don't stand on ceremony here."

At school, we just automatically called all of the adult males "sir". It was the SOP (Standard Operating Procedure) of the school system. The men in positions of authority were all "sir", the women were all "miss". This was going to take some getting used to.

"Yes, si...I mean, Jo-Jo," I said

"Cain's quite enamored with you," he said.

"He is?" I mean, I thought I felt something, some kind of...chemistry whenever we were together, but it could be projecting, like we'd learned in SAP class (And wouldn't my teacher be proud I'd recognized it as that?). Anyway, I thought I was projecting, thinking he liked me because I wanted him to so badly.

"Uh-hmm," he said in affirmation. "He highly recommends you for the job."

"Uh, Jo-Jo?" Calling a man so much older than me by his first name, especially when we'd practically just met, sounded as foreign rolling off my tongue as it felt to hear it.

"Yes, my dear?"

"I don't want to sound ungrateful, because believe me, I really want the job. My family could really use the money, but..."

"Yes?"

"What exactly is the job I'm interviewing for?"

Jo-Jo laughed, sounding more self-deprecating than as if he were laughing at me and my question. "I run a business here. I do desktop publishing, for lack of a better term, designing stationery, web pages, advertising, and the like.

"I have many customers from my generation, hold-outs to the old way of business. They virtually insist on paper trails." He gave a loud guffaw there, and then said, "Did you see what I did there? I described my old-school paper trail using the word, 'virtual'. I believe that's what you call a paradox, is it not?"

I forced a smile, feeling incredibly out of place. I looked around Jo-Jo's office. There wasn't a computer or digital device to be found. Even the telephone on his desk was this weird, black, behemoth phone, its buttons arranged in a circle as if it were a retrofitted dial.

Jo-Jo must've noticed me looking, because he said, "You like my phone? Damn phone service went digital a few years back and my dial phone wouldn't work anymore. One of my kids brought me this one to replace it. It's quite an elegant solution for an old-fashioned Luddite like me, don't you think?"

"I'm sorry—what's a Luddite?"

"Someone who shuns technology."

"But you said you made web pages."

He slid a drawer out from under his desk and tilted the laptop resting there so I could see it. He put it down and stroked the Apple logo on the top of it as if it were a pet. "It's a necessary evil in the twenty-first century. I've developed a love-hate relationship with it. I curse the technology, but it's my bread and butter, so I can't throw it on the floor and stomp on it."

I smiled awkwardly, unsure if he were joking or not, took a deep breath, and said, "About the job?"

"Yes, yes. The Job." He said it just like that, as if it should be spelled with capital letters to emphasize how important a position it was. Jo-Jo slid the computer drawer back under his desk and rolled his chair up against the desk until the edge of it seemed buried in the rolls of fat at his midsection. "I need someone I can trust to deliver printed materials to the clients who have ordered them."

"But...I don't have a car."

"No matter." He pointed to his temple with his index finger. "There. I've made a mental note to send you to places easily accessible by TTC."

"But—"

"You're probably wondering: why not use Purolator?" He paused, nodded once, winked, and continued before my brain could formulate an answer. "My customers prefer the human touch."

I thought to tell him that humans deliver for Purolator, but decided against it.

"I told you earlier: we're a bunch of old fogies who long for the olden days—milk trucks and bicycle couriers, and the like.

"You know your way around the city?"

"Yes, sir."

"Uh?"

"I mean, yes, Jo-Jo."

"Perfect. You're hired."

"That's it? That's the whole interview?" Though I hadn't been on many interviews before, I was sure there should be more to it, like asking about my grades at school or my past experience or something, even if I knew how to ride a bike.

"I'm a good judge of character, and your reference is impeccable."

"Thank you," I said. I started to get up to leave.

"Don't you want to know more, like how much it pays, and when you start?"

I felt stupid. "Yes," I said sounding calmer than I felt. I sat back down. "Of course I do."

"Cain will take you to get a Metropass. I'll cover that for as long as you work for me. Cost of delivery will vary depending on size of package and distance you'll have to travel. Most deliveries average anywhere from ten to twenty dollars. And I pay cash on the barrel, in case you're wondering, tax-free.

"Sound like a plan?"

Twenty dollars a delivery? Seeing as you can get pretty much anywhere in the city in an hour, that meant less than minimum for around two hour's work, but if it was tax-free?

"It's a deal," I said.

Jo-Jo reached a hand out over his desk for me to shake. When we were done, he passed me a pen and paper.

"What's this?" I asked.

"Standard non-disclosure agreement. People who do what I do are few and far between, as are people like my clients. I want to be sure my employees don't give away any of my trade secrets, or 'lose' a package because my competition pays them more." He made air quotes around his head when he said the word "lose".

I signed his paper. "I didn't realize the world of desktop publishing was so cut-throat," I said, trying to make a joke.

"It's a crime what this world's come to, isn't it?"

CHAPTER EIGHT

What was in the package?" Jem asked. We were walking to the corner Timmy's to grab something for lunch. I'm addicted to half Dark Roast, half Hot Chocolate, and I was PMSing, and craving it badly.

"I don't know," I said. "Business cards?"

"Are you asking me or telling me?"

"Who are you, Judge Judy?"

Jem stopped dead in her tracks. I continued on for a few metres before I realized she'd stopped. "What are you doing?" I said. "We have to be quick. I can't be late to Ballbuster's class." Ballbuster was my period three English teacher. She *hated* when kids strolled in late from lunch and absolutely refused to help us catch up by telling us what we'd missed. If we deigned ask for help for the rest of the period, she reminded us that maybe we should make more of an effort to get to class on time next time, like punctuality was the key to knowledge or something. It certainly seemed to be the key to access *her* knowledge.

"Forget Ballbuster. I can't believe you delivered a package for this Jo-Jo guy—whom you just met—without finding out what you were delivering first."

"Can we just drop it? Any more of this sedentary yet scintillating conversation and I'm going to have to wait for my drink until after school."

Sedentary: staying still, like the early Canadians when they set up their villages, grew crops, and built longhouses.

Scintillating: as in the way stars sparkle (and the word that had killed my chances at winning in the lunchtime spelling bee during last month's Spirit Week festivities).

Jem rolled her eyes. She let me pull her along, providing some resistance for a few steps before she gave it up and fell into step beside me. I let go of her wrist when I was sure she was going to keep up. "This is serious, Jude. I watch *Border Security*. I know that sometimes you get caught for nothing more than being ignorant."

This time *I* stopped. "So I'm ignorant, now?"

"That's not what I meant and you know it."

"Then what *did* you mean?" I mean, I love Jem and all, but I hated that she was making me feel stupid. I finally had a job. I had money in my pocket that wasn't in my father's first. Wasn't that supposed to be a good thing?

"I mean ignorant as in trusting. As in not having street smarts, or having street smarts but not using them." We just looked at each other for a few seconds, neither one of us seeming to be sure what to say that wouldn't serve to aggravate the situation further. Jem was my best friend. I didn't want to fight with her, and this was beginning to feel like a break-up.

"I just mean...how much do you really know this Cain Guy?"

Jealous much? Jem didn't even *know* Cain. What could she possibly have against him except that he'd been taking up time that I'd ordinarily spend with her?

She hooked an arm around mine and started to pull me forward. "Tell me again what happened on your delivery. All of it. Starting from Jo-Jo."

I walked with her because now I also wanted a Boston Cream so badly I didn't care if I walked into Ballbuster's classroom with chocolate on my lips, yellow pudding on my nose, and Dark Roast-slash-Hot Chocolate dripping down my chin. "Jo-Jo sent me with Cain to get a MetroPass. When we were done, Cain gave me a cardboard box. I knew Jo-Jo had a publishing business, so I assumed it was either, like, invitations or business cards, because the box was small, you know?

"Cain gave me an envelope..."

Cain gave me an envelope and said, "Your pay. Open it when you're done. Or before, if you need it." He asked for my phone and then asked me to unlock it.

"Why?"

"So I can beam the address to you."

"My phone beams?"

He laughed, something that sounded more self-deprecating than mocking of my lack of tech knowledge, and said, "It does." His turquoise eyes sparkled. He flashed his dimples at me again, and my stomach tumbled.

He held his phone against mine. When he separated them, he dropped his phone into his lap and leaned over toward my side of the car. "Google Maps," he said. "Tap on the address and it opens.

"Now, you're travelling by TTC, so click the bus icon and it will give you directions. Click here and it goes step by step. You can follow your movements on the map as you go. It's near impossible to get lost. If you make a wrong turn, click here and the map will re-calibrate." He smiled at me again, only this time he also winked. He could have told me the sky was green with purple polka-dots at that moment in time, and I would have believed him.

"If by some crazy quirk of fate you do get lost, click here to dial my phone and I'll talk you through it." He leaned over even closer and kissed me on the lips, and I felt as if my bladder might burst.

I didn't know what to do. My heart sped up and I thought I might panic, but then my lips started to move as if on their own, following his. It did nothing to quiet my heart. The butterflies in my stomach and the beating of my heart seemed to take my breath away, but in a good way, as strange as that might seem.

"I've got your back, Jude. I wouldn't let anything happen to you," he said, and I believed his conviction.

He gave me back my phone and moved his phone from his lap to the cup holder between us. "The important thing is to go there, get in, deliver the package, get out, and go home."

I nodded once, with purpose. When I opened the car door, Cain reached for my hand and squeezed.

"One more thing: don't hand it off to anyone except for the guy in your phone. Not his secretary, not his assistant, but him personally."

"Got it," I said with another firm nod.

He squeezed my hand once more and I was off.

I didn't tell Jem all that stuff about the kiss, or Cain's eyes, or his dimples, because I knew what she'd say. Instead, I just told her about the MetroPass, the envelope, the twenty dollar bill inside, and how Cain knew to beam the information from his phone into mine.

"Go on," she said.

"I found the place okay—some law office on Bay Street. I went in, asked for the guy expecting the delivery, and left it with him."

That wasn't entirely true. Like Cain said, I met his secretary who'd insisted I could leave the package with him.

I refused.

He said the guy was in a meeting. I channelled my inner Joan Watson from *Elementary* and said that I'd wait.

The guy came out a moment or two later. When I handed him the package, he handed me another envelope.

I asked him what it was for and he told me it was my tip. When I opened it on the bus ride home, it contained a ten-dollar bill.

I told Jem about the tip.

"I still don't trust That Cain Guy. Or Jo-Jo, for that matter."

"That's because you don't know them."

We went into Timmy's and ordered our food, which we ate on the walk back.

"How are we doing for time?" I asked her.

"We're good."

We walked a few more steps in silence and then Jem said, "Do me a favour?"

"For you? Anything." I said.

"I'm serious."

"So am I."

"The next time Jo-Jo gives you a job to do, call me before you go."

"Why?"

"Aren't you even the least bit curious to see what's inside the packages he gets you to deliver?"

I shook my head. "I told you: I trust Cain."

"And by default Jo-Jo, I got it. But you trust me, too, right?"

"Of course."

"So you'll call me then?"
I agreed that I would.

CHAPTER NINE

Cain called early that Saturday and woke me up. I answered my phone with a groggy "Hello?"

"You're not still sleeping, are you?"

"What?" I closed my eyes and felt myself drifting off again. "What time is it?" I asked, sounding to myself as if I were underwater. I took my phone from my ear and read the time. "Six-fifteen?" I said into the phone when it was back at my ear. "I like you Cain, but not enough to have a coherent conversation at six-fifteen on a Saturday morning.

"I'll call you when I'm up for real."

Cain chuckled. "You can't. That's why I'm calling. Jo-Jo's planned a retreat and I'm going."

I sat up in bed, suddenly awake. "A what?"

"A retreat. You know, a bunch of us getting together to hang and do things."

"Have fun," I said. I tipped my head back until it rested on my headboard and closed my eyes.

"No, Jude, Jo-Jo said you should come with."

It killed me to turn him down, but I said, "I can't today. Dad's off work and we're supposed to grab lunch and a movie."

"Can't you postpone it? Your dad'll understand."

"We've barely spoken in...I don't know how long. This was supposed to be our day." I hated that I sounded like a whiney brat, but it was true. Mom was dead, so it was a given that I'd miss her something awful. But Dad was still there, and if there was one takeaway from Mom's death, it's that I never want to take him for granted.

"You're always saying how he worries because you don't have any friends. I would think he'd be glad you'd want to ditch him for some new ones."

Spending the day with Cain *was* tempting, but let's face it: chances are my dad would be there a whole lot longer than Cain would. I didn't need to have experience with boys to know that teenage ones were fickle and that my days with Cain were numbered.

Did that mean I should go with Cain because he might not be around for very much longer, or go with my dad because he would be around a whole lot longer than Cain?

It was way too early in the morning for an internal philosophical debate.

"Talk to him. For me," Cain said, and I could imagine his bright green puppy dog eyes pleading.

"I'm not promising anything, but I'll talk to him."

"When?"

"Soon."

"Do it fast, 'cause I'm in your driveway waiting."

"How'd your dad take it?" Cain asked as I belted myself into the passenger's seat of his car.

"Bittersweet."

"He'll get over it."

"That's kind of mean."

Cain put the car into reverse to back out of the driveway. When we were on the road he said, "Dad's are supposed to be like that, forgiving. Or so I'm told."

"What do you mean?"

"Just that...I never really knew my dad. Or my mom, for that matter."

"Cain! I'm sorry."

He forced a smile and shook his head. "No biggie. That's just the way it is."

"Tell me."

"You don't want to hear my sob story."

His hand was resting on the gearshift. I reached over and took it in mine. "Isn't that what a relationship's about? Sharing sob stories?"

Cain let out a breathy, self-deprecating laugh.

"You already know mine: dead mom, working dad, no friends, blah, blah, blah. It's only fair you tell me yours."

"You sure you want to know? I mean, once I share my origin story with you, you're forever bound to hold my secret. It also makes you vulnerable to any arch-rivals who might take you out to get to me."

"I think I can handle it," I said with a smile.

"My dad used to drink—"

"Oh, Cain, I'm sorry—"

"It gets better. He used to hit my mom. She just...took it. Better he take it out on her than on me, she used to tell her friends on the phone when it got rough. Except one day he *did* take it out on me, and we took off to a shelter, but he found us."

My stomach grew sour just listening to him tell a story I couldn't even begin to imagine. And he told it so matter-of-factly, too. My eyes still teared up whenever I thought of my mom, and I was prone to becoming a bawling idiot if I ever had to tell *her* story. I was in awe of Cain, not his story, but the way he told it, with such full-on inner strength, that I could almost believe he was some sort of superhero in disguise. You'd kind of have to be, living through something like that and coming out like him on the other end.

"By the time the police got there, the social workers had him subdued. He was arrested, tried, and convicted, and that's all she wrote."

"Where's he now?"

Cain shrugged. "I have no idea. And I plan to keep it that way."

"And your mom?"

He shrugged again. Something in his demeanour, something in the way he held his head, the way he gripped the steering wheel, told me he needed to get it off his chest, but that he didn't want to burden me with it. Almost as if he were afraid it might change my opinion of him if I knew.

"Mom lost it. It's like she couldn't come to terms with the fact that she couldn't protect me, like even when she did what was best for me, it backfired, and he came looking for us."

"Where is she now?"

"She had a breakdown. She was never the same after that. I think she's in a halfway house somewhere in the city, but I haven't heard from her in...years."

"What happened to you? Who took care of you when she had her breakdown?"

"Child and Family Services. I bounced from foster home to foster home for a while. I met Jo-Jo when I was fourteen, and he saved me." His voice grew almost reverent when he said this, which was kind of creepy. "Jo-Jo became like my surrogate father. He even tried to foster me at one point, but he was too old, or too poor, or too single, or some other stupid thing like that.

"Jo-Jo gave me a leg up. He gave me a job, gave me advice, taught me right from wrong." He looked over at me then and said, "I know it sounds cliché, but I seriously don't know where I'd be now if Jo-Jo hadn't have found me."

"You poor thing," I said. Cain always seemed so put together, so...in control. It was hard to believe his life had begun so chaotically.

"See?" he said, kind of angered. "That's exactly what I didn't want to happen."

"What?"

"Pity."

"I don't—"

"Is Superman to be pitied for being saved when Krypton blew up? Is Spiderman to be pitied for being bitten by the radioactive spider? Is Batman—"

"Okay! Okay. I get it." I let go of his hand and reached over to touch his cheek. He took my hand from his cheek and kissed it.

"And just for the record, Batman's a horrible example."

CHAPTER TEN

We drove for quite a few kilometres in silence, me digesting what Cain had just confided, and Cain...I suppose Cain was thinking about the same thing. He was probably wondering if he'd just dropped the deal-breaker on me. I know, because I was wondering the exact same thing. Cain was my first boyfriend, and he was broken, like, to the max. Was that what I wanted for my very first relationship?

It's like when my mom used to tell me about how she and Dad met. Nowadays, all sorts of people meet online, but there was no online when my parents were young, so they went to an old-fashioned dating service, like a glorified matchmaker. Mom was adamant she not be fixed up with someone who had been divorced. The lady at the company tried to talk her out of it, but Mom told me she didn't want anyone who came with that much baggage. And while I'm not naïve enough to assume that whomever I wind up with won't have some sort of baggage of his own, did I really want to be with someone who came with that much of it?

Cain reached over, turned on the stereo, and played some sort of weird, falsetto-voiced, disco tune.

"What's this?" I asked.

Cain looked over at me as if thinking I was questioning him about an object I was holding. He looked back to the road and said, "Oh, you mean the music? It's the Bee Gees."

I couldn't help but giggle; my dad had the Bee Gees on the stereo in his car, too. "How *old* are you, I mean, really?"

He smiled. "Let's just say Joj's influence goes further than my well-being." He clicked to the next song. "Better?"

I recognized the song. *Save a Prayer* by Duran Duran. Every time Dad heard one of their songs he told me the group was like Mom's One Direction growing up. He also told me she used to sing this very same song to me, when she rocked me to sleep when I was a baby. "Better," I told Cain, though I didn't go into why.

We went back to travelling in silence for the remainder of the song. In the quiet between tracks I asked, "Where are we going, anyway?"

"This place. Joj tries to find a different place each time, so each one's a new experience. That way, even the unfamiliar becomes familiar, 'cause we're doing something familiar in it." He takes a quick look over at me. "It sounds better when he says it."

"No," I said, feeling this huge grin grow on my lips. "That's beautiful." And it was, and romantic, and tender, and sweet. Not so much coming from Jo-Jo, but the fact Cain had chosen to quote that exact thing at that exact moment, and that he had chosen to quote it to me. I reached over, took his hand, and squeezed. He squeezed back and flashed me that smile, the one famous for turning my legs to rubber bands and setting the butterflies in my stomach aflutter.

When we turned off of the highway, it was to drive down a two-lane, poorly paved road in a rural area. I was amazed that farms still operated so close to the city. Growing up, there were a few of them close by that we used to go to and buy or pick fresh fruit and vegetables or pies they made with their produce. I watched as, over the years, they slowly disappeared to be replaced with strip malls or condos. The last of the farms was just sold over the past year. Gone were the days I'd drive past to see freshly sheared sheep in the yard when the weather warmed.

Cain must've been on the same wavelength, because he said, "Amazing, isn't it? When I was a kid, everything north of Highway 7 was farmland, and now? Don't get me started."

I told him about the last holdout I knew of, the sheep farm, and he gave brief, breathy, "Ha!" Then he said, "And people complain about the seven dollar cauliflower. Dumbasses."

Wow, this walk down memory lane had turned dark quick.

"And pollution and traffic..."

He looked over at me again, put a hand on my knee, and squeezed. "Sorry, Jude. Let my inner-activist out there for a minute. I promise to lock him back in his cage for the rest of the day."

"Don't do that on my account," I said. I put a hand on top of his hand and forced my fingers between his. "You're right," I told him, hoping he'd think we were simpatico. "I mean, everything you eat or breathe is bound to kill you. If the preservatives don't get you, the fish DNA in your fruit will." I hoped he didn't think I was talking out of my ass, because I essentially was.

Cain pulled his hand from mine and put it back on the wheel.

"What?" I asked, thinking it was because he knew I was bluffing and thought I was stupid.

"We're here." He flashed me his knee-weakening smile once more.

74

We parked outside of this huge building that looked more like a mansion than a house. "What *is* this place?" I asked.

Cain shrugged. "Joj said there was some rich guy who died and left his property to the province on the condition it be made into an outdoor education and conservation centre. This used to be his house."

"I can't imagine ever living in a mansion like this; it's huge."

"Babe, compared to how I grew up, living in *your* house is like living in a mansion."

I felt awful. I tried to focus on the fact that he'd called me babe, but I couldn't help the way I grew up. My parents worked hard to get the house of their dreams, and my dad's practically killing himself to keep it.

Did Cain really begrudge me my upbringing? Was he somehow jealous?

"Sorry," Cain said. He put a hand on my shoulder and squeezed. "That was unfair. Can we rewind and try again?" He smiled and showed me his dimples, and all I wanted to do was kiss each of them. His teeth were so incredibly straight and white, I wondered if he'd ever worn braces.

I nodded and forced myself to return the smile, but my safety metre went down by a few notches as a result of the experience. What was I doing there? What was I doing with Cain?

Jem's words came back to me: how much did I really know This Cain Guy? Not much at that point, but I was getting to know him, more and more each time we met.

The question I had to ask myself was if I liked what I was beginning to know.

He had a lot of baggage due to his childhood, but he seemed okay despite it, thanks to Jo-Jo's intervention. Still, it seemed as if he still had quite a few unresolved issues, as evidenced by his comment about my house.

He cared for the environment and the economy, but harboured some anger there, as evidenced by him calling people dumb asses.

So far, Cain came out about even on my list of pros and cons.

"Hey," Cain called to me. He'd made his way to the front door in the time I'd been lost in thought. "Coming?" He held his hand out to me.

I nodded, smiled a genuine smile, and closed the distance between us to take his hand. I wanted to trust him. My hope was that I'd be able to gag my inner Jem and know, once and for all, that Cain was safe by the time we'd settled in for the drive home.

CHAPTER ELEVEN

Inside, the building was darker than I'd expected, even though it was lit entirely with fluorescents. The floor had these beige and grey linoleum tiles that made it look a bit dirty. There was a wall of cubbies under the wooden staircase off to my left, and I got the idea this was where they'd welcome school groups when they went on those overnight bonding and character-building outings, like we did in grade nine.

Jo-Jo met us a moment or so after we'd entered the building, and said, "You're just in time for lunch." He held his hand out for both of us to shake and then turned to take a step back toward the room at the end of the hall. When he got to the door he said, "Come...come. Cain, you're with me. Judith, I've sat you at table number three, with some other girls your age."

His words hit me like a slap in the face. I looked over at table number three to see the two home wreckers from the other day and thought I'd empty my bladder right there. I looked at Cain, reluctant to leave him, but he flashed me that dimpled smile, winked, and said, "I'll meet up with you after lunch." He left me standing there, trying to get up the courage to face my trial by fire.

The "girls my age" Jo-Jo had sat me with turned out to be the home wrecker girls from the other day, the same one who had been sitting on Jo-Jo's couch, trying to goad me into a fight. Rather than scrutinize and pick during lunch, they did something else bullies are known for—ignore and shut out, which was fine with me. Why, in a million years, Jo-Jo would ever think I'd be okay to sit with Cain's ex and her friend is beyond me.

Maybe it was a test. If I emerged intact at the other end of the meal without begging Cain to take me home, then I was worthy as a mate for his surrogate son. I kept my head up, focussed on my meal, and bided my time taking small bites and counting forty chews with each one. The plan was that either they'd finish before me and leave or Jo-Jo would emerge to put an end to the torturous meal.

During the Salem Witch Trials, women had rocks tied to them and they were thrown into water. If they floated, they were proclaimed witches and killed. If they sunk, however, they'd passed the test, and the townspeople would frantically try to save the women before they'd drowned—if they were lucky.

Was this scenario designed for me to sink or float?

Cain, I knew, wanted me to float.

The real question was: what did Jo-Jo want?

If I sunk, then it would be up to Cain to jump in and save me before it was too late. This might work in Cain's favour, as he'd emerge as my knight in shining armour in the scenario.

If I floated, then maybe I'd be angry at my situation, or maybe realize I didn't need Cain as much as Jo-Jo would have liked.

But Jo-Jo liked me, I argued. Otherwise, why would he have hired me the way he did?

When, at last, Jo-Jo stood, he said, "Shall we retire to the den?"

People stood slowly and followed him out of the large mess hall in single file. Though I'd barely finished my sandwich at the time, I was grateful to get back to Cain, who met me at the door on my way out of the room.

"That was painful," I whispered. We follow the mass exodus from the mess hall to the room Jo-Jo had called the den.

"Was it really that bad?"

"Not if you like eating like a monk."

Cain laughed. "Ouch!" he said, mockingly. "Give them time. They'll come around."

"Given their icy reception, I'm not sure I want them to."

"Don't be like that," Cain told me.

He took my hand and drew me into the large meeting room that looked like it might have been the original Great Room of the house. At least as large as the mess hall, the room was totally panelled in dark wood. There were a number of seating areas set up in various configurations and combinations of couches and easy chairs, or wooden chairs with tables between them, making the room look more like a Starbucks than the living room of a century-plus, old home.

Jo-Jo was already seated in a large armchair in front of a huge fireplace at one end of the room. When I say huge, I mean *huge*. I think I could have walked into it and stood straight up without scraping my head on the top, if there wasn't a fire going in it, that is. It was weird, because there were about thirty people in that room, and not one of them went up to speak with Jo-Jo. He just sat there in the antique armchair, wearing this silk robe, like what they used to call a smoking jacket when Ricky wore them in the *I Love Lucy* repeats I watch with my dad. He had a huge ring on his finger, too. The scene was almost surreal, as if he were a mob boss waiting for someone to pay him tribute.

Cain motioned for me to sit on some pillows that had been placed on the floor so he could go and speak with Jo-Jo.

"*You* don't be like that," I said.

"What am I like?" He said this with a chuckle, which I didn't like. I was being serious and expected him to be, too.

"*I'm* not the problem," I said, pouting a bit.

"I never said you were."

I felt him kiss the top of my head. "The only problem I see here is that I have to sit next to Joj during his speech. You'll be okay on your own, won't you?"

I didn't want to be left alone, primarily because besides Cain and Jo-Jo, the only other people I recognized were the home wrecker girls. I nodded anyway. I mean, what else could I do? Tell him that I was a wuss and afraid those girls would start up with me again?

"Good," Cain said with a wink.

Jo-Jo looked up at Cain when he got to his side. Cain knelt in front of him and squeezed his ring hand, which connoted (I pay attention in Media class, too) a whole bunch of Mafia movie scenes where the gangster pays fealty to the don by kissing his ring.

But that was stupid, right? I mean, Jo-Jo wasn't even Italian. And though I'm not naïve enough to think there aren't mobs in all cultures—in case you haven't already noticed, I *do* watch television, you know—the scenario fit, but it also didn't fit.

The man was a graphic artist, for goodness' sake.

Even the most famous of Mafioso had their covers.

I was appreciative Cain chose that moment to divert my line of thinking by calling the group to order. Before then, most of the people in the room had been milling about, getting reacquainted with those they hadn't seen in a while. Either that or reinforcing existing cliques, gathering in groups of two or three in the corners or around the furniture, and keeping to themselves.

Case in point: the home wrecker girls were leaning on a window sill, whispering to each other, pointing with a nod of the head or the flick of an eye, and giggling.

Still others were loners like me, sitting on random pillows strewn in a rough circle on the floor in front of Jo-Jo. I wondered if they were first-timers as well.

"We're ready to begin," Cain said with a clap of his hands. He nodded to me, and I nodded back, relieved he hadn't forgotten about me and my insecurities.

Cain sat, and Jo-Jo stood. The group seemed to bow their heads as if in awe of his magnificence. The scene was discomfiting, to say the least.

"Welcome, everyone," Jo-Jo said, holding his arms out wide, as if reaching out to give everyone in the room a hug. "Thank you to the wonderful staff here for the extraordinary lunch."

Campbell's tomato soup and white bread, grilled cheese sandwiches. Far from what I would describe as extraordinary, but then again, I was a guest, and beggars can't be choosers.

"The meal in which we have partaken was totally organic and non-GMO."

Unlikely. That meal was my go-to comfort food. After Mom died, Dad stopped buying bakery-made challah in favour of Wonder Bread. Grilled cheese was still good, but it wasn't the same as when Mom used to make it. Unless he'd dropped a pretty penny for the tetra-packs of cream of tomato soup they sell in the health food section of the supermarket and figured out a way to get the same texture from fresh bread as the ones they make with the preservatives, that meal was anything but healthy.

What was Jo-Jo's game?

"For years, food producers have been splicing fish DNA into our produce, telling us it'll help lengthen its shelf-life. Scientists are experimenting with meat grown in a test tube with an eye for human consumption, and we're supposed to just eat it and believe them when they tell us it's safe.

"Our doctors prescribe designer drugs to prevent people from feeling the effects of the kinds of things our grandparents and their parents before them accepted as part of a normal life.

"It's only a hop, skip, and a jump before we're consuming *human* DNA spliced into our food, seeking out drugs to keep us unfeeling, and using stem cells to genetically alter the path of human evolution."

This comment was followed by a number of hear-hears from the crowd. Though I didn't hear him say it, I saw Cain's jaw move, and I knew he was voicing his approval, too.

"It's time we return to a simpler time, vow to say no to GMOs, preservatives, and stem cells."

The timbre of Jo-Jo's voice raised a little as he spoke. "It's time to show Big Business, Big Pharma, and Big Tobacco their days on this earth are numbered."

There were some yesses vocalized by the crowd.

Jo-Jo's voice rose further until he was almost shouting. "It's time to put an end to them before they put an end to us!"

Some people pounded the floor at this statement while others stomped. Cain clapped loudly.

"This weekend retreat represents a return to simpler times. We will work as our ancestors did, tilling the fields, shunning electricity, spending our leisure time by firelight."

Jo-Jo nodded to Cain.

Cain stood, went to the front door, and came back with a large wicker basket in his hand.

Jo-Jo continued, "No electricity means no electronics, people. Check everything with brother Cain."

Brother Cain? Given their relationship, I'd have thought he'd refer to him as "my son" instead.

There was a long silence as everyone watched Cain meander through the people in the room. Everyone he approached dropped their cell phones into the basket. When he got to me he said, "Hand it over, babe."

I looked up at him and kind of pressed my lips into a frown.

"It'll be fun. You'll see." He lowered the basket so I could see the others' devices inside.

I'd read online how there have been studies into the withdrawal people experience when they forget their cell phones at home. My dad always has his cell on him, but he seems immune to the phenomenon. Whenever he forgets his cell at home, he laughs it off, but I do notice he spends an inordinate amount of time on those evenings checking his social media.

Reluctantly, I put my cell in the basket, too.

When he returned to his seat, there was a frenzied moment in which I thought he was going to toss the entire thing, basket and contents, into the fire. Instead, he sat the basket down in front of the fireplace and resumed his position on the pillow beside Jo-Jo's throne.

"First world vices," Jo-Jo said with a quick, breathy laugh, and most of the crowd did the same. It sounded more like a muffled guffaw, as if the people in the room were already losing their marbles, having been un-jacked from their social media.

"Fully one-third of all food grown in North America goes to waste," Jo-Jo preached, "and people are starving all over the world, including some in our own backyard.

"Our landfills are full. We have nowhere to send our garbage, and we still live in a throwaway economy, doubling the commercial packaging of our goods, throwing all sorts of things into the trash." Jo-Jo paused again as if to survey the sea of teens through twenty-somethings in front of him to see if he still had the pulse of the crowd.

"We take designer drugs to prevent us from feeling, drugs that our bodies cannot fully break down, drugs that wind up in the sewer system, drugs our water purification systems cannot eliminate, drugs that wind up back in the water supply, which we ingest one more." The way he delivered his speech was nothing short of expert showmanship, like those carnies whose job it was to pull people into the sideshow tents, or the roadside snake oil salesmen, like the Wizard in the black and white scenes in *The Wizard of Oz*.

"Society favours cheap materials instead of the biodegradable, green, and sustainable ones because they cost a bit more," he continued. "We add abrasive plastic beads to our toiletries that wind up in the water table, poisoning our lakes and oceans and the wildlife calling them home.

"If science has progressed to the point where it can—" his voice cracked here "—take stem cells from aborted fetuses and use them to further prolong our lives, why can't it figure out a sustainable way to preserve the environment? This is the question I propose you keep in mind as our festivities progress today."

Festivities?

Tilling fields? Shunning electricity? Leisure time by firelight?

Maybe we were going to brush our teeth with abrasive toothpaste and compare how many of the blue, plastic beads lingered on our gum lines. Or better yet, preserve ourselves from the inside out with the GMO and preservative-laden cold-cuts they were sure to serve for dinner.

Jo-Jo continued, his voice even louder than before. "We are weekend warriors, grassroots gladiators, sovereign soldiers, with a single goal—the betterment of the environment. By hook or by crook, we will make a difference!"

The room erupted in a muddled chorus of hear-hears, yesses, grunts, and floor pounding, which escalated until the whole room was chanting Jo-Jo's name. Cain seemed to be the loudest of them all. Jo-Jo's assertion that we would shun electricity aside, the energy in the air was electrifying, and I was caught up in it, in spite of myself. Before I knew it, I was chanting Jo-Jo's name and beating the floor with my open palm in time to the chant.

At one point in the midst of the elated spirit, I looked up to Cain. It took a moment, but our eyes eventually met, and a smile grew on his face, the likes of which I'd never seen before, it was that wide. Pride beamed from his eyes, so bright and strong I had to look away. When I'd found the courage to look back, his gaze was focussed elsewhere, but that look of pride at the lather he and Jo-Jo had stirred up inside the room remained plastered on his face until Jo-Jo dismissed us.

CHAPTER TWELVE

During the break, Cain and I found a quiet place off the beaten path. We sat beneath a huge maple tree, our backs leaning against its mammoth trunk, and Cain took my hand in his. All was silent, save for the tweet of birds overhead and the chirp of the odd cricket, but then I said, "Why am I here?" It's something I'd been wondering since he'd plopped me down at that table with those girls.

Cain took a breathy laugh and said, "I don't understand the question."

"Why me? Why bring *me* here?"

"Do I have to say it?" He sounded almost hurt. "I thought the way I felt about you was kind of obvious."

"I mean, *why* do you feel that way about me?"

Cain leaned forward so I could see his face. "You're not just fishing for compliments, are you?"

"I'm serious."

"Wow!" he said, leaning back against the trunk. He also let go of my hand, which made me think I'd blown my only chance at happiness. "I don't know." He paused for a beat and then said, "How do I love thee? Let me count the ways—"

"I said I was serious, Cain." I shifted my position until I was sitting with my legs bent and out to my side, my back away from the tree. "I have these teeny, beady eyes, a hook nose, and I could stand to lose a good ten pounds. Why pick me?"

"Huh."

"What?"

"Nothing, I...I just thought you were different."

"Different like how?"

"Different like you weren't into that self-hating, I don't look like a supermodel crap."

"I know I don't look like a supermodel. Supermodels don't look like supermodels without their hair and makeup and Photoshop. I'm just...call me a realist."

"Okay. I think you look healthy. Your weight," he poked me in the stomach like I was the Pillsbury Dough Boy or something, "is perfect for your frame. Your nose," he touched the tip of his index finger to the tip of my nose, "is in perfect proportion to your face. And though your eyes aren't big and round, they *are* the perfect colour, like...of the ocean. No, wait! I can do better.

"They're the colour of the sky at sunrise on a cloudy, stormy day."

"Thanks...I think." I shifted my position again, until I was a little closer to him, cross-legged, our knees touching.

"It gives you character, like there's more going on in there than just a pretty face."

"What, no sonnet?"

"Shall I compare thee to an autumn's morn—"

"That's not Shakespeare."

"Nope." He chuckled and my heart did a flip-flop in my chest. "It's a Barrett original."

There was a lull in the conversation and then I said, "What about those other girls?"

"What other girls?"

88

"Those ones from the house the other day. They like you."

"Well, I don't like them."

"Not anymore."

Cain hesitated before answering. "What do you mean?"

"I just got the feeling there was something there once."

"There was. I told you as much the last time you asked."

"Both of them?"

He hesitated again. "I suppose."

A horrible thought crossed my mind. "At the same time?"

"Is that what you think of me?" He sighed and said, "Look, it's like I said: I dated one of them and then we broke it off. You know teenage girls; they find it hard to separate their problems from those of their friends, like when their pheromones sync their periods they become psychically linked or something."

Now it was my turn to hesitate. "That's not funny."

"I wasn't trying to be. How about we just drop this one? It's over now. I've moved on, and you should, too."

We sat there for what seemed like an eternity in silence. Again, I wondered if I'd just blown my entire relationship with him, but then he took my hand and held it, rubbing my fingers with his thumb.

"Do you believe what Jo-Jo said back there?" I asked him.

"I think he has some valid points."

I waited a few minutes, trying to figure out how to broach my concerns. Cain loved Jo-Jo as a father; I didn't want to say anything to insult him, let alone drive Cain away. "What Jo-Jo said? It scared me."

"It wasn't supposed to generate the warm fuzzies."

"I mean, the environment's screwed, I've always known that—all you have to do is look at the last winter we had to know something's up, and it's only going to get worse when you consider the global warming denial the president's preaching in the States—but the way he made me feel was the same as I did in 2012, when the Mayan calendar ended."

"And how was that?"

"Like doomsday's upon us." He slid his fingers between mine and squeezed. "Like if I go to bed tonight, there'll be nothing to wake up to tomorrow."

Cain brought my hand to his lips and rubbed them with one of my knuckles. "There's this meme on the Internet—you know what a meme is, right?"

"Yeah. They're those pictures with the sayings on them."

I felt Cain's lips smile beneath my finger. "Close enough. Anyway, there's this one meme that says something like we don't inherit the Earth from our parents, but we borrow it from our children. Doomsday, as you call it, won't come in our generation, or probably even in our children's generation. But our children's children?"

"Our grandchildren."

Cain nodded. "Yep. *They'll* have something to worry about."

"Unless the government unleashes a super-flu before then."

Cain nodded again. He rubbed my knuckle against his lips again and then brought our hands down to rest on his leg. "See, that's Jo-Jo's point."

I chanced a glance at him and he looked at me, too. He smiled and winked. "Famine? Genetic engineering? Reluctance to change the infrastructure to make way for better fuels? These are things that'll get *us* in our lifetime, and yeah, our kids and their kids will suffer the fallout, but it's like Gandhi said, *we* have to be the change we want to see in the world."

Wow. First Shakespeare, then the meme quote, then Gandhi...either Cain was one heck of an enlightened guy, or he's learned to tow Jo-Jo's company line.

"Cain?" I asked. I hesitated to finish because I didn't want to burst the Jo-Jo bubble Cain was floating on. I also didn't want him to think I hadn't drunk the Kool-Aid, I mean, no-guy—except for maybe my dad—ever looked at me the way Cain did back in the Great Room. When I was chanting and he was smiling at me, it was this smile I can only describe as beatific (beatific: a blissfully happy smile as if in holy bliss, like the girls who'd said they'd seen the Virgin Mary in the sky at Fatima on that TLC documentary Dad was watching). First, his mouth opened, extending the bow of his lips and showing the tips of his teeth. Then his dimples took form, bracketing his mouth like dark parenthesis beneath the scruff on his cheeks. From there, it spread upward to the apples of his cheeks, and then to his eyes, where faint crow's feet formed. His eyes brightened—imagine dark pools of matcha latte with sparkles thrown in and stirred, so they flickered in the light. No way I wanted to lose that feeling. It was intoxicating. I wanted to experience it a thousand times more.

"Yep," he said.

"Do you trust Jo-Jo?" It was a stupid question, I know, and it wasn't exactly what I wanted to ask him. I was worried. What if Jo-Jo was trying to do something more self-serving than unite kids to better the world? What if he was fear-mongering? What if he got off on the attention?

"Implicitly." He let go of my hand and sat up straight. "He saved my life, Jude, I told you that."

"I know, but—"

A bell sounded, not quite a bell—more of an electronic beep, reminiscent of the fire alarm in my school.

Cain stood and so did I. He smiled at me, but it was just a regular smile, barely putting a dent in his dimples, and I thought my lunch might soon come up. I'd ruined it, I knew I did.

"Time to get our afternoon assignments," he told me. He put a hand on my shoulder and squeezed. "Talk later?"

I nodded.

He pressed his lips together and firmly nodded once in response before taking my hand and leading me back to the old mansion.

CHAPTER THIRTEEN

T he rest of the afternoon was spent exactly how Jo-Jo said it would be: tilling the fields. He'd volunteered us for random jobs in the conservation area. Some of the kids were assigned to plant flowers in front of the house, or to tend the vegetable and herb garden out back. I was given an orange vest, a canvas bag on a metal hoop, and a long pick, dropped off at the side of an access road near a parking lot, and told to pick up garbage on my way back to the house. I felt (and looked) as if I were part of a chain gang—minus the chains. Before the van drove off, Cain handed me a water bottle through the front window—a *plastic* water bottle.

"Stay hydrated," he said with a wink. He nodded to the driver who drove off. When they were a few yards away, the driver beeped the horn, twice, in two, quick toots. The sensation I was being punked washed over me.

I wanted to do a good job, nevertheless. I wanted him to give me that beatific stare again, the one that made me turn away because I'd meant so much to him I couldn't stand it, so I picked up garbage as I walked back toward the house.

It was a good deed, a *mitzvah*, at the very least.

About ten minutes in, I cracked the lid on the water bottle, recalling what Jo-Jo had said about landfills, that we were making garbage faster than we could dispose of it. Dad hoarded cases of plastic water bottles in the basement, but we weren't allowed to drink any of it. He was keeping it in case there's a problem with the water, like what happened in Walkerton, Ontario in 2010, or in case the power went off, like in the summer of 2003. After that, he went out and bought a generator. I think a part of him secretly hoped something like that would happen again so he'd get a chance to actually use it.

I took a swig from the bottle and added it to my list of growing paradoxes where Jo-Jo was concerned.

He preached non-GMOs and a healthy environment, but he served us garbage, preservative-laden food, and sent us short distances in gas-guzzling vans. He condemned our throw-away culture, but provided his volunteers with water in single-use, plastic bottles.

I suppose it could have been worse—he could have dropped me off with no water at all.

Dinner was spaghetti with bottled tomato sauce, and garlic bread on the side. The garlic topping was so salty and yellow, I knew it was that margarine-based, garlic spread stuff they sold in tubs at the supermarket. After Mom died, Dad went on a sort of health kick and refused to buy margarine any more, saying that the manufacturing process was only a single step away from the manufacturing process of plastic. He told me it was like making whipped cream—if you put whipping cream into a bowl and begin beating it, eventually you would have this creamy mixture that was amazing in strawberry shortcake, but if you continued to beat it, you'd eventually be left with butter. Therefore, whipped cream was one step away in the manufacturing process from making butter. One was great on chocolate cream pie, the other, not so much.

When you ate margarine, you were essentially eating the container in a softer form. Therefore, what we were eating was garlic-flavoured plastic—chemicals—on white flour bread that would probably last in a landfill longer than I would. If, that is, you could find the landfill space in which to dump it.

Jo-Jo stood at the end of the meal to thank the staff for our day. When he was done, Cain came to get me at the table. I could almost feel the darts the home wrecker girls opposite me were aiming at my back.

Cain held a hand out to me and said, "Shall we?"

I nodded, took his hand, and let him pull me out of the chair. He curled me into his arms and hugged me. I giggled, more for show than because I was giddy, I have to admit.

After I'd buckled my seat belt, I said, "That was...interesting."

"Feels good to know you've done some good in the world, doesn't it?" He turned the key in the ignition.

That wasn't exactly what I was going for, but all right.

"We do that sort of stuff all the time. Community service. Cleaning up the environment."

When we'd left the parking lot and were on the road, I said, "Doesn't it strike you as odd that Jo-Jo said—"

"What?" He looked over to me, his eyebrows knitted together, as if in concern. A shallow furrow formed in the middle of his forehead and I imagined how he might look in twenty or thirty years, when the furrow had deepened.

"It's just..." I took a deep breath, unsure how to continue or if I even *should* continue. "He's a little...antithetical, wouldn't you say?"

"I'm not even sure I know what that means."

"You know, like...paradoxical."

"What's that?"

Seriously? I mean, thesis and paradox are like, grade nine English stuff. I took another deep breath and said, "Like, he doesn't walk the walk."

Cain laughed, which wasn't the response I'd expected. "You just don't know him yet," he said.

I chanced a glance at Cain because I was worried I'd blown it again, but when Cain chanced a glance back at me, he was smiling. "Those kids back there wouldn't know organic or GMO from their backsides. I think Jo-Jo does it to test them. I think he's just waiting for someone to call him on his crap, and the fact that you have means you're even more valuable to the organization than either he or I had imagined?"

"So, it was a challenge?"

Cain shook his head. "More like a game." He took his hand off the wheel to scratch his chin. It sounded like sandpaper on wood. It made me want to reach out and test if it made the same sound when I did it.

"He knew you guys wouldn't call him out on it to his face, but he told all of us to report back to him if you said anything to us in private."

"And I passed?"

"With flying colours."

We drove for a moment in silence. Cain turned onto the highway. When he'd gotten into his lane and matched the speed of the other drivers, I said, "Cain?"

"Yup."

"Who is us?"

"Huh?" He looked over at me quickly and then turned his attention back to the road.

"You said he told all of you, all of *us*, to report back to him. Who do you mean when you say, us?"

"The recruiters."

I felt sick. Was that all I was to him? A *recruitee*? If that was the case, then there was something seriously cray about their recruiting practices.

"Look," he said. He reached over, grabbed my hand, and squeezed. "I told you I was a recruiter. This is what I do for Jo-Jo: find him people he can bring into his organization." He rested our hands on the gearshift.

"And that's all I am?" I was fighting back tears at that point. "A recruit? No wonder those girls resent me if this is how you do it." I tried to pull my hand from his, but he tightened his grip and refused to let go.

"Oh, Jude," he said. He turned to give me a lascivious look. "You are so much more than just a recruit. You are *the* recruit."

I hated him. I mean, in that moment, I *really* hated him. I felt used. I felt humiliated. I tried to pull my hand from his once more, and he tightened his grip even further. In a voice that was nearly a whisper, I said, "What's that supposed to mean?"

Cain chuckled, deep and throaty. "I was joking, Jude, lighten up."

"That's not funny."

"You were never a recruit, Jude. I wanted to get to know you from the moment I saw you, but I didn't know how to approach you, so I fell back on the recruit patter."

"I find that hard to believe," I said.

Now he did let go of my hand. "What do I have to do to prove it to you? What if I pulled over right here and shouted it out to all the drivers as they passed by? What if I pulled over right here and *showed* you how I really feel?"

He looked over at me. I said nothing, but crossed my arms over my chest.

"Fine. You leave me no choice. Just know that whatever humiliation I am about to endure, it's on you." And he put his signal light on.

"What are you doing?" I asked.

"I'm pulling over."

"Why?"

"I just told you." He changed lanes.

"Where are you going to go?"

"I'm going to pull over onto the shoulder near one of the traffic cameras and profess my affection for you. The cameras are going to record it and it will be picked up by CP24 and broadcast so the whole world will know how I feel."

"You don't have to do that."

"I want to."

"I believe you."

He reached over and turned the signal light off. "Tell me what you believe."

"Really?"

He flipped the signal light back on again.

"I believe you when you say I'm more to you than just a recruit."

He turned, flashed me his dimples on the ends of a huge smile, clicked the signal off, and merged with traffic into the next lane on his left. When he'd matched the speed of the other cars, he reached over and grabbed my hand again.

We drove about a kilometre in silence and then I said, "Don't you want to know how I feel about you?"

I turned to look at him and saw his grin in profile. "I believe I already do."

CHAPTER FOURTEEN

Cain turned off the 401 in Mississauga somewhere. When I asked him where we were going, he grinned and said, "You'll see."

I wasn't scared; more like curious. Cain often did this to me, not filling me in on the details until the last minute, and though so far it had meant I ate crappy food and had to pick up someone else's garbage, there was something invigorating about it—the helping to keep the conservation area clean, not the food. Wherever we were going, I knew there was some kind of silver lining to it. It might be a bit tarnished and I'd need to Anne Shirley it a bit—you know, polish it up in my mind—but it would most likely be there.

We pulled into the parking lot of a big box grocery store. It was late and the store was closed, so the parking lot was mostly empty. Cain drove around the back of the store and stopped in front of the dumpsters. Another of Jo-Jo's recruiters was waiting for us in a pick-up truck there.

Cain got out of the car and so did I. He went around to his trunk and gave me a pair of rubber gloves, the kind you see on television that people wear to protect their perfectly manicured fingernails when they wash the dishes. He held out a dark green, canvas onesie and said, "In or out?"

I felt my mouth drop open and I stared at him, trying to form the words.

"The dumpster," Cain said. "In or out?"

"You're going into the dumpster," I said, more of a statement than a question.

"Unless *you* want to, yes."

"What on earth for?"

"Yo, tell her to keep her voice down, dude," the other recruiter said.

Cain ignored him. "You heard Jo-Jo: food waste. People only want perfect produce at the height of ripeness. Food depots throw away a *ton* of food, produce in particular, because they're not perfectly symmetrical, or they're over ripe, or spotted. What makes it to the store is what people want, but then it gets jostled in the truck or sits on the shelves and the stores have to throw it away. The only thing this serves to do is drive up the price of fresh produce."

"Can we postpone the marketing lesson until after we're done?" The other recruiter seemed super nervous and jumpy.

Cain shook his head at him and continued. "The food banks want non-perishables, and they're pretty good at rounding it up and redistributing it, but the one thing people need is fresh produce. Chances are someone patronizing a food bank isn't going to be able to afford fresh produce." He nodded at the building behind us. "This store dumps their spoiled produce twice a week. Today is one of those days."

"But if it's spoiled—"

"Spoiled is subjective," Cain said. "Most of it's still edible, if you peel back a few leaves or cut off the brown spots. Joj sends us out to collect whatever's salvageable—you know, no maggots or slime—"

"Gross."

"And he sees to it that it gets into the hands of the people who need it."

"Look—can we just get on with it?" the other guy said. "Every second we're out here is another we can get caught." At least I knew why he was so jumpy.

"I thought that once you throw something out you're giving up ownership of it," I said. I knew this was how reporters got information about famous people, for example, by going through their garbage. And it was legal. "Why would anyone care if we're here?"

"What's in the dumpster is free game. Being on the property could be construed as trespassing. Technically, the parking lot's private property."

I started to get nervous, too. What Cain was doing, what *we* were doing, *could* be counted as another *mitzvah*. And while I didn't think the police would just up and arrest us for trespassing without a warning, judging by Recruiter Two's behaviour, I could only assume he'd been warned before. If caught again, the police might not differentiate between first time and repeat offenders and simply arrest us all. Needless to say, that was something I wanted to avoid.

"Oh," I said. What we were doing was kind of exciting, I have to admit. I'd never done anything even borderline illegal before, and it came with a kind of rush. "I choose out, then."

Cain nodded and started to wriggle into the green suit. "I'm going in," he said. "Wish me luck."

I smiled at him and said, "Luck."

"That's the best you can do?"

I smiled again, went over to him, and kissed him chastely on the lips.

"Not what I was hoping for, but it'll have to do." Cain smiled.

"Can we just get on with it, please?" Recruiter Two said. "You all can get a room and continue—" he wagged a finger at us, "whatever this is later."

Cain climbed into the dumpster. It seemed only half-full, because he was still standing quite high once inside. At one point he squatted and I heard him rummaging around. "Eureka!" he called.

Recruiter Two nudged my arm. When I turned toward him he was holding a plastic grocery bin, the kind you buy at the supermarket to carry your groceries in instead of using a bag. I took it from him, and he said, "Your boyfriend's going to pass you food from the dumpster. Your job is to put it in the crate. When the crate's full, you give it to me and I'll give you another crate and stack the full one in the truck. Got it?"

"Got it," I said with a nod.

Before long, Cain started handing me food, armfuls of it, some of it still in its packaging, like the hearts of lettuce, or berries, or grape tomatoes. Some of it had mould, especially the berries, but I'd taken stuff like that out of our fridge umpteen times before. If you pick out the spoiled berries, you can still eat the ones untouched by the mould.

By the time we were done, we'd filled at least a dozen of those grocery bins.

Cain climbed out of his suit and threw it into the dumpster along with our yellow gloves. He turned to me and said, "Now, kiss me like you mean it."

"I'm out," Recruiter Two said.

A moment later I heard his truck pull out of the alley, leaving us in the dark.

We stood there kissing away the adrenaline for a while, before Cain broke the embrace and said, "It's getting late. I should get you home."

It was almost ten by the time Cain pulled up in front of my house. I'd hoped the house would be dark because Dad had gone to sleep, but no such luck. Though most of the house was dark—Dad's a stickler for turning off switches when you leave the room—the flicker of the television was coming from the front den window.

And I thought I was nervous back when we were dumpster diving.

CHAPTER FIFTEEN

"**C**rap," I said.

"What's wrong?"

"My dad's still up."

"I'll leave you to him, then," Cain said. He handed me back my cell phone. I was so caught up in the events I'd forgotten it wasn't still in my purse. "Jude? What we did today? What we did tonight? You can't tell him."

"I don't understand. We did good, right?"

Cain shrugged. He looked so serious, that furrow in the middle of his forehead made an appearance. "Jo-Jo's orders. He likes to keep his work under wraps, like Batman, or Robin Hood."

His analogy was cute, and I smiled in spite of myself. He kissed me goodnight with a quick peck on the lips, squeezed my hand, and let me go. He drove off before I'd even finished crossing the street.

Dad must've heard the porch door open, because he was at the front door before I'd even had the chance to unzip my purse. The first thing he did was to grab me and hold me tight. Then he pulled me inside and locked the door behind me. I expected a tirade at that very moment, for him to yell, wave his arms, tell me I was grounded, but he turned and walked away instead, without saying a single word.

"Are you okay, Dad," I asked, following him into the kitchen at the back of the house.

Dad didn't answer.

"Dad? Talk to me."

"No, Jude," he said coolly. "*You* talk to *me*." He rinsed his tea cup in the sink. "Where were you?" he said, his back to me as he focussed on the water coming from the faucet in the sink.

I shrugged, which I know he didn't see, because he seemed to be making a concerted effort not to look at me.

"I thought we were going to spend the day together," he said.

At this point, I feel the need to clarify. I lied. To Cain. I told him Dad was cool with me skipping our plans, but he obviously wasn't.

He actually didn't know I was cancelling until he woke up.

I left him a note. That's probably why he was so angry.

"Was that today?" I said, trying to deflect.

"Don't mess with me, young lady," Dad said. Now he did turn, but he left the water running in the sink. "We talked about it last night. How many tomorrows did yesterday have?"

"You're right. I messed up."

"Where were you?" He reached over and turned off the water in the sink. When he looked at me, I read extreme disappointment in his eyes. He looked haggard in the bright, white light of the fluorescents, and I suppose he was, assuming he'd been sitting in front of that television set, making phone calls in an effort to locate me all day. "And before you even think of lying I know it wasn't with Jem, because she's worried sick, too."

Cain had cautioned me against telling Dad where I was. He didn't say I couldn't tell him *whom* I was with.

"I was with a boy," I said.

"A boy?"

I nodded.

"Does this boy have a name?" The only indication I had that Dad was barely holding it together was that his voice cracked when he spoke.

"Cain."

"Cain. Last name?"

"Barrett. His last name's Barrett." I figured it was okay to spill the beans about Cain because he's got a teeny tiny digital footprint, so Dad couldn't look him up, even if he tried.

"Where did you meet this Cain Barrett?"

"At the mall."

"He's a mall rat?" Dad has this thing about my not becoming what he calls a mall rat, someone who does nothing with her time but sit around the mall sipping lattes and chilling. He blames it on the economy, and on the psychology of Gen Xers. It's a long story; he saw a documentary about it. He does that all the time. He sees something or reads an article and feels immediate and present danger for me. I hate it when he tells me about it, too. It's like he doesn't trust me, or thinks I'm an idiot.

"He works there," I told him. It wasn't a lie. Cain did work there; he worked *at* the mall, just not *in* it.

"Where?"

I shrugged.

"You don't know where he works." He said this as more of a statement than a question.

"I don't know. Somewhere in the Food Court, I think." It wasn't an outright lie. Considering what we'd done that day—dumpster diving to salvage food for the hungry—he's feeding people, same as if he'd worked in the Food Court. "He told me where, but I forgot."

"Where at the mall did you meet this boy?"

106

"Food Court." I wondered if that was too suspicious—Cain worked at the Food Court and I met him at the Food Court, but I couldn't recall where in the Food Court he worked.

"You let yourself get picked up by some boy in the Food Court?" Apparently, not suspicious at all, because Dad's mind glossed over the whole Food Court confusion to launch into his Don't Meet People Online In Person tirade. "Did you meet him online?"

"No." And what if I did? Yes, there are predators online, but so am I. So is he. So are most of my schoolmates. Why does the fact that people talk online automatically make them predators?

"Don't lie to me, Judith."

"I'm not, okay?" That's another thing—Dad always thinks I'm lying, even when I'm telling the truth. "I met him at the Food Court."

"Well, you might as well have met him online, for all you know about him."

"You don't know that."

"I do. I was a teenage boy once, remember?" Oh, here we go again!

Dad took a deep breath, walked over to the kitchen table, and sat."What *do* you know about this Cain boy?"

"Enough."

He'd been looking at his hands folded into a ball on the table in front of him, but then he looked up. "What's that supposed to mean?" he said.

I was getting madder by the second. "It means you're never around and it gets lonely around here and you can't expect me to have to rely on Jem for companionship, twenty-four-seven."

He paused and kind of squinted at me. "How dare you?" he said, barely a whisper. His voice gradually rose as he spoke. "Do you think I like what I'm doing? Working as much as I do for as little as I get? The only reason I do what I do is because of you, so you'll have certain advantages, like a roof over your head, clothes on your back, and food in your belly."

"Don't do me any favours." I knew I'd crossed the line as soon as I'd said it, but you can't unspeak something, especially something as hurtful as that.

"Don't you talk to me like that. If this is what you're learning from That Cain Guy—"

"What? You'll forbid me to see him?"

"For a start."

"I'd like to see you try." It sounded challenging. It *was* challenging. My stance when I'd said it—legs shoulder-width apart, hands on my hips—was challenging. I was tired. I may have smelled. All I wanted was for that day to be over, especially then.

Dad took a deep breath. "This conversation is going nowhere," he said. "Before we say anything either of us will regret," as if we hadn't already, "I'm going to bed. When you're ready to apologize and speak to me with respect we can continue this conversation, but not before." He got up from the table and walked past me. "I expect an apology from you in the morning," he said as he passed.

He was about halfway up the stairs when he said, "You should call your friend to tell her you're home. Maybe then at least one of us'll be able to sleep soundly tonight."

CHAPTER SIXTEEN

I went to school early the next day and waited for Jem at her locker.

"Stalk much?" she said when she was near. She grabbed her lock and dialed in the combo.

"Hey," I said.

She looked at me for a moment, sizing me up, as if trying to decide if she should respond. Finally, her expression softened and she said, "Hey."

"Are you still talking to me?"

"Barely."

"Seriously, Jem. Are we okay?"

"Maybe," she said. She refused to look at me, busying herself rummaging through the stuff in her locker instead.

"Could you just *stop* talking to me in sentence fragments, please."

She shrugged her shoulders. I liked it better when she was talking in fragments. At least then she was talking.

Then she did look at me. "What you did, Jude? Not cool."

"Those are still fragments."

Jem shook her head. She looked as if she was stifling a giggle, or at the very least, a grin.

"Stop that," she said. "I'm pissed at you, Jude."

Bad that she was angry. Good that we were back to full sentence terms.

"I'm sorry," I told her, and I was, like, really, *really* sorry.

"Just...give me the heads up next time, okay? Then I could at least say you were in the bathroom or something, and text you to call him back."

"I promise. Next time—"

"There's going to be a next time? *So* not cool, Jude."

I shrugged. I mean, I hoped there'd be a next time. Not necessarily going to one of Jo-Jo's retreats, but spending the day with Cain.

"Where were you, anyway?" she asked. She closed her locker door, clicked the lock into place, and spun the dial.

I shrugged. Cain said not to tell anyone. Actually, what he'd said, just before I'd left his car, was that I couldn't tell *him* about what we did. But Jem wasn't him, meaning my dad.

Cain also said Jo-Jo likes to keep things under wraps, like Batman, or Robin Hood, but Robin Hood had his Merry Men and even Alfred knew of the existence of the bat cave.

Jem gasped. "You were with *him*, weren't you?"

I nodded shyly as we turned the corner into our first period class.

"I don't know if I like This Cain Guy, I mean, your dad was worried *sick*—"

"Cain didn't know." We settle into our seats at the back of the class. Jem and I didn't originally sit together because the teacher had a seating plan, but one day, during a work period, I moved next to her and the teacher didn't say anything, so we figured it was okay. We'd been sitting at the back, side-by-side, ever since.

"What do you mean?"

"I told him Dad was cool with it, and then I snuck out and left him a note."

"When did he find the note?"

"When he woke up, I guess."

Jem shook her head. "Do you want your dad to hate Cain? I mean, he's never going to believe you did that on your own."

I shrugged. "Right now he's not talking to me, so I don't know what he thinks."

"That's serious shit, Jude."

"I know," I said, louder than I'd intended. Some of the other early birds in class looked over at me, and I ducked my head and said it again, using my inside voice.

"He wants me to apologize first."

"What did you say to him?"

I shrugged. I'd said some really hurtful things that I'd rather not discuss while sitting in class and waiting for the morning bell with my friend, who I'd gotten caught up in the whole sordid affair, and who'd just recently decided to forgive me.

"He thinks Cain's like this offline predator who singled me out."

"Huh," Jem said. She opened her binder and started flipping pages.

"What's that supposed to mean?"

"What? Oh, nothing."

"You said, 'huh.' It means something or you wouldn't have said it." There was a noticeable lull in the noise level in the room because I'd raised my voice again.

"It means huh, like an exhalation of air."

"And..."

"And nothing."

"And it means *something*. Tell me what."

Jem fished a pen from her pencil case and started copying down the day's agenda.

"Jem!"

"Nothing," she said.

"Jem!" I pulled the pen from her hand.

"Great, Jude," she said, pointing to the mark the pen had left when I grabbed it. She went back into her pencil case, took out a cartridge of correction tape, and started to cover it up. When she was done, she held her hand out for the pen.

"Tell me," I said, holding the pen at arm's length and out of her reach.

"Just that...maybe...he is."

I practically threw her pen onto her binder, slumped back in my seat, and looked away. I didn't want her to see the tears welling up in my eyes—what she'd said had stung even worse than Dad forbidding me to see Cain again.

She must have noticed my posture, because she said, "Look, all I'm saying is that you should be careful. I mean, you meet him in the mall when you're looking for a job and he just happens to have one for you. He sends you on these errands across the city with these sealed packages, and now he convinces you to stand your father up and leave him some kind of Dear John letter—"

"I told you: Cain knew nothing about the note."

Jem nodded. "Fair enough."

I blinked away the tears, wiped the ones that escaped from my eyes with the palm of my hand, and turned to face her. "What can I do to convince you Cain's okay?"

Jem shrugged. The bell rang. The *William Tell Overture* started playing through the loud speaker.

"What did you guys do together, anyway?"

"I don't know...stuff."

"Like...adult stuff, or kid stuff?"

"Stuff stuff."

"Thanks, Jude. That's very helpful."

112

The *Double-Jeopardy* theme played next.

I exhaled loudly. "We went to a conservation area to pick up garbage. Community service stuff."

"Does Cain have a record?"

I turned to look at her with an exaggerated smile. "What, like, a vinyl record? Yes. In fact, he played them all for me on the portable turntable in his car on the way to the conservation area."

Jem looked at me with a frown. "You know what I mean."

"Why do you ask?"

A deep voice came over the PA saying, "Please stand for the national anthem," followed by a series of chair scrapes. Teachers called to tardy students in the hall asking them to stop moving until after the anthem and announcements were over.

"Just...ex-cons do community service. Maybe it's what he's used to doing on the weekend, so he thinks it's a cool thing to do on a date."

The teacher shushed us. She'll allow us to sing during the anthem but not to speak.

When *Oh Canada* was over, there was a scheduled moment of silence. Jem and I exchanged sideways glances at each other throughout, waiting until we could speak again.

The PA voice said, "Please be seated." This followed by more chair scraping and the daily announcements. Once more, the noise level in the class grew. The teacher shushed us, like she does every day (sometimes she throws in an "I can't hear the announcements," if we're really loud), but no one really listened.

"Ha ha," I said, sounding droll. "Very funny."

"I wasn't trying to be funny, Jude." She looked at me again and said, "When are you making your next delivery for him?"

"I don't know. He hasn't asked me to do it yet."

"When he does, call me. I'll meet you, and we can check it out together."

"Cain usually drives me to the subway."

"So I'll meet you in the subway. On the platform. Text me before you go so we can time it."

I didn't know what she hoped to accomplish by accompanying me on a delivery, but for the sake of our friendship, and so she'd stop fantasizing worst case scenarios about me and Cain, I agreed.

"Jude?" she asked. "How deep are you in with Cain?"

The announcements had stopped by then and the teacher was going over the agenda.

"What do you mean?"

"I mean, is your relationship still platonic?"

Platonic. As in intimate friendship. I guess that might describe us.

The teacher started reading the attendance roll.

Then again, intimate could mean so many things. I mean, Jem and I are platonic. We're also intimate in that we've shared our secrets, hopes, and dreams. Cain and I were intimate, too, but on a different level. We held hands, kissed, and cuddled, but not intimate in the way a man and women are when they're alone. I hoped that, one day, Cain and I would share our secrets, hopes, and dreams, but for now?

Now I knew little of Cain. I knew he'd had a rough childhood, that he was close to Jo-Jo, and that he did charity work. I knew I was prone to getting lost in his eyes, and that one day I might like to lick his dimples, but were we a watered-down version of platonic, or intimate in the true sense of the word?

"What kind of a question is that?" I asked.

114

"Just that...you didn't go anywhere or do...any*thing* to compromise yourself, have you?"

"I promise you that if I do, you'll be the first one to know."

Whether or not I'd actually share that moment with Jem, when and if it happened with Cain or anyone else, I wasn't sure, but it seemed to satisfy her.

"Pinky swear?" she asked.

I smiled. "Pinky swear," I said. We entwined pinkies and let go, just as the teacher began her lesson.

CHAPTER SEVENTEEN

Cain was waiting for me when I left school. He'd parked across the street and was standing in the road, leaning against his car with his legs crossed at the ankles and his arms crossed over his chest, looking like a final act, John Hughes, boy prize. Cue the eighties' soundtrack, I thought, and was admittedly disappointed when I didn't hear Simple Minds or The Psychedelic Furs.

When he saw me, he smiled, lifted a hand from his chest to wave, and then crossed his arms again.

My heart beat double-time, but I managed to return both the smile and the wave. When I grew near enough to smell his cologne, he stood upright, put his hands on my shoulders, and kissed me.

"What are you doing here?" I asked when our lips parted.

"Jo-Jo has a job for you."

My heart dropped in my chest, still unsure if I wasn't more to him than a recent recruit for Jo-Jo's courier service. "And here I thought you missed me," I said, half mock-pout, half real-pout.

"*That*, and Jo-Jo has a job for you."

I eased my backpack from my shoulder and held it near the ground at arm's length, grateful to

116

redistribute the weight. He took it from me, opened the back door, and tossed it into the back seat.

"I don't know, Cain. I mean, my dad was real mad last night."

"You said he was cool with, you know, us spending the day together."

"Yeah. About that—"

"Oh, Jude, you didn't." The features on his face went lax, as if he were disappointed in me.

"I'm sorry," I said. "It's just...he was so looking forward to it. I thought this was the best way." He might have sacrificed the day if I'd planned to spend it with Jem, for example. No matter what, he'd never agree to my spending it with a boy, let alone an older boy—really more of a man—and one he'd never met, to boot.

"Jo-Jo's rule number one: if you can't lie by omission then don't lie."

"But I kind of did that. I omitted telling him I was cancelling our plans to spend them with you."

He harrumphed. "That's not the same, and you know it," he scolded. He looked at me from under his eyebrows, frown obscuring his dimples. "Let's go."

In the car he said, "You're not grounded, are you?"

"No, I'm not."

"Because if you're grounded, it wouldn't do any of us any good to piss your father off even more, not you, not me, not Jo-Jo either."

"I'm not grounded, okay?" I said, giving him a bit of attitude. Who did he think he was, anyway? Even if I *were* grounded, it wasn't any of his business unless I decided to *make* it his business.

"Let me get this straight—you took off on your dad without telling him, disappeared for the whole day with a boy he doesn't know, and there were no consequences?"

117

"Who are you—my parole officer?"

"I'm serious, Jude. We have to be careful. The last thing we need is for your dad to forbid you from seeing me. I won't play Romeo to your Juliet."

I sighed. "The only consequence is that he's not talking to me. Not until I apologize, which I plan to do when he comes home tonight."

"You're sure?"

"I'm sure."

"Because we all know how it wound up for Romeo and Juliet."

"I'm sure. Can we just...let it go?"

Cain turned the key in the ignition and put his hand on the gear shift as if he were about to put the car into drive. Instead, he dropped his hand back into his lap. When he turned the car on, the radio started to play something modern. It was a far cry from my John Hughes soundtrack ideal.

"I care about you, Jude. I don't want to do anything that's going to jeopardize our friendship." He reached across the gap between the bucket seats and took my hand in his.

"Is that what we are?" I brought his hand to my mouth and kissed one of his knuckles, looking up at him from under my eyelashes. "Friends?"

Now he smiled. It was a huge one, eye sparking, tooth baring, and full on dimple showing. "You *vixen*, you."

Vixen? Did he mean like Santa's reindeer? A female fox? The comic book character?

He looked at me and shook his head. "The delivery; you up for it?"

"Let's go," I said.

He dropped my hand, shifted the car into gear, and drove me to the subway station.

The instructions were specific: the envelope was to go to a lawyer's office mid-town. Barring delays in the subway system, it should take me anywhere from fifteen to twenty minutes to get to my stop, about the same amount of time to walk to the office, and ten minutes to drop it off—about an hour in total. Given the time Cain picked me up, and the time the office closed, there was little time to waste.

"Get in, get out, go home," Cain said to me. "No time for dawdling, at least, not until after you've made the delivery." He handed me the sealed, manila envelope, and a second, legal-sized, white envelope. "Payment and directions inside the second envelope, as usual." He smiled at me again. "Any questions?"

I shook my head. "Simple enough. Get in, get out, go home."

"Text me later, kay?"

"Kay." I got out of the car and went into the back seat to grab my backpack. Instead of leaning over to get it, I slid in to sit in the back seat. "When will I see you again?" I asked.

He looked at me through the rear view mirror. I couldn't see his full face, but faint crow's feet formed in the corner of his eyes, and I knew he was smiling. "Soon enough."

Once I'd entered the tunnel to the subway, I fished my cell phone out of my purse and texted Jem, as promised.

Surprise delivery. U in? I texted. My thumb hovered over the icon in the corner of the monitor, an orange circle and the cartoon image of an envelope pierced with an arrow, feeling caught between a rock and a hard place.

If I texted Jem, was I betraying Cain? Did I risk not making the drop and jeopardizing Jo-Jo's reputation? How might that affect Cain's relationship with his surrogate father?

Jem was convinced Jo-Jo—and Cain by default—were up to no good, that they were setting me up for something. If I didn't text her, I'd never hear the end of it.

I didn't know how my relationship with Cain would end, if Cain was The One, or how many people I'd date before I'd found The One, but I imagined that however it ended, Jem would be there to pick up the pieces.

Sisters before misters, I told myself, and hit the send button.

It didn't take long for Jem to respond.

I'm in. Where R U?

Subway. Finch Station

Meet on platform?

Hurry. On deadline. Can't miss office closing

On my way now. 20 mins tops

CHAPTER EIGHTEEN

We jumped onto the subway as the chimes rang, seconds before the doors closed. Practically before the conductor eased off the break, a canned, female voice came on the loudspeaker to announce the next stop would be North York Centre. The ride south was pretty vacant—most people were riding home north during rush hour—so Jem and I could talk pretty freely and with minimal voice raising.

"You got the package?" Jem asked.

I looked around. Though the subway was nearly empty, there were still people around. Any one of them could have construed that question in any number of ways.

I nodded, emphatically.

"Let's see it."

"Not here."

"Why not?"

"I don't want anyone to see. Not here."

"But no one's here." Her voice caught a little on the word 'but', and it came out as almost a giggle.

"Still."

We rode the rest of the way to the first stop in silence. When the doors closed again and the announcer said the next stop would be Sheppard

Avenue and that it was a transfer junction, Jem said, "Where are we going again?"

"Bay Street."

She nodded. "The Financial District."

"Huh?"

She shrugged. "I don't know. That's what they call it on television. You know, because that's where the Stock Exchange is."

I thought of my grandfather and how he'd always had a ring-bound map book in his glove compartment. He treated it like his bible or something. God forbid any of us ever opened it roughly and bent one of the pages or even worse, ripped one. The cover was red plastic. *Perly's Maps*, I remember it was called. "Thank you, Perly's," I said.

"Huh?" she said.

"Nevermind."

The next station came and went. When the doors closed again, I said, "So what are you going to do with the package when we get there?"

"Open it." She said it just like that—plain and simple, as if she should be following it with a "duh" or something, like I should have known all along that was the plan.

"You can't open it."

"Why not?"

"It's sealed."

She patted her backpack, resting on her lap.

I snickered. "What? Do you have a kettle in there or something?" I'd seen umpteen shows on the Disney Channel where the kid knew the letter from her school was the bearer of bad tidings, so she tried to steam it open to check out the contents before her parents could.

"I have my ways," she said with a smile.

Silence again until the subway came to the next stop, picked up and dropped off passengers, sounded chimes, and went on its way.

"What's the story with This Cain Guy, anyway?" she asked me.

"There's no story. He's just a guy."

"A guy you've fallen for, head over heels."

"It's not like that."

"Then tell me what it *is* like."

I shrugged. How could I tell her how Cain made me feel? How he made me realize that I never was alive until I'd met him? How when I'm with him, I feel as if my first sixteen years were only play-acting? "I don't know." I paused. "He makes me feel...special."

"There are other ways to feel special than having sex with a guy, Jude."

"Jem!" Her name came out as a sort of whine and a bit louder than I'd intended it to. "It's not like that, either," I said, much quieter.

"So far you've told me a whole bunch about how it's not, and nothing about how it is."

"God, you're impossible," I said, kind of breathy. "It's like...he makes me feel pretty...wanted—"

"Your dad wants you. *I* want you."

"Yes, and I love you for that, but it's not the same." I turned to look at her and had to look away. I couldn't just throw my heart and soul on the table for her to scrutinize and watch her face as I did. It's like when you write a poem or short story in English class and you have to peer edit—I can't just stand around while the person reads my inner-most thoughts like that. And even though it was Jem I was talking to, it kind of felt the same way.

"I feel loved by you and my dad, but this isn't the same. It's the way he looks at me, like he's craving my company or something—"

"It's called sex, Jude."

"Stop saying that!" I said that too loud, but this time I'd intended it to be. "This is not about sex. Cain and I haven't had sex yet, and we're not about to anytime soon."

"He's older than you, Jude. He's practically a grown-ass man. Boys have needs—*men* have needs."

I shook my head. My eyes burned as if I were about to cry. "Stop saying sex, *please!*" I chanced a look at her, and she looked a bit concerned. Her eyebrows knit together and a frown-line formed on her forehead between them.

The subway stopped again. Someone got on and sat in the seat next to Jem. She wriggled over a bit closer toward me. I looked up at the people in the car and noticed it was growing a bit more crowded. I guess the farther south we went, the more people we picked up who either lived downtown or who needed to catch a Go train at Union.

"He does things. *Charitable* things. He makes me feel as if my life matters—"

"You matter to me. You matter to your dad—"

"This is different. On one of our dates we picked up trash at a conservation centre, and then we rescued food from a dumpster to give to the homeless."

"Right. Because the homeless deserve to eat someone else's garbage."

"The food was newly placed there. Stuff at its peak ripeness or just expired. It's good, healthy food that would otherwise go to the landfill." I looked over at Jem who was shaking her head as if in disbelief. "Doing that? We killed two birds with one stone because we saved garbage from going to the landfill *and* fed the homeless.

"When I do stuff like that with Cain? It makes me feel powerful, like I can make a difference."

124

"He's brainwashed you, Jude."

"Is it brainwashing to make me feel empowered?" My eyes burned with anger. How dare she? Cain was the best thing to happen to me in, like, ever. Why couldn't she see that? "Is it brainwashing to make me feel like I can make a difference? Like I matter?"

Jem was looking at the backpack in her lap at that point. She closed her eyes momentarily. When she looked up at me, she looked scared, and I wondered if she feared she might lose me as a friend. Truth be told, I was wondering the exact same thing in that moment. "You matter to him as long as you keep delivering packages for that Jo-Jo guy."

That was a low blow. I looked back at her, my lips pursed together of their own volition. "That's not fair."

"We'll see," she said. "The proof's in the pudding, Jude. We'll see when we open the package."

We travelled the rest of the way to Bloor station in silence. Other than calling directions to each other so we wouldn't get separated, we didn't say much as we transferred subways, or as we searched for the address on the package Cain had given me.

CHAPTER NINETEEN

We arrived with time to spare before the close of the workday.

"Let's get this over with," I said, meaning let's drop this off and get home before Dad does.

"The way I see it, we have two choices," Jem said. "We can open it in the subway john, or find one in a building on the surface."

"That again?"

"That was the deal, wasn't it?"

I knew exactly what she was talking about and I cringed inwardly. I was dying with curiosity to know what, exactly, Jo-Jo needed me to deliver, but I couldn't shake the feeling that taking a peek inside meant I was somehow betraying him. More importantly, taking a peek inside meant I was somehow betraying Cain. Just the thought of it made me sick to my stomach.

"What deal?" I asked.

Jem gave an exaggerated sigh. "I help you open the package before delivering it to prove, once and for all, Cain's intention is to use you."

I felt my cheeks grow hot at that statement. "And here I thought you were going to open the package to prove Cain only wants to help me out because he loves me." I forced a smile. "Funny, isn't it?"

126

"Hilarious."

Now I actually wanted to open the package, if for no other reason than to prove Jem wrong. I told myself that Jem was jealous I'd grown so close to Cain recently, which meant I'd grown further away from her. "Let's go." I took her hand and we went to the surface, saw the building we were looking for, and jay-walked across the street as soon as the coast was clear.

"Bathroom," I said when I saw the sign.

"Not on the main floor," Jem said. "Somewhere less conspicuous." She went to the wall panel listing the offices in the building. "Is there a proper basement here?"

"There's an x-ray clinic there."

"That's where we'll go to do it."

We took the elevator down and found the bathroom. Inside were three stalls. The far one was a handicapped stall slash baby change station.

I followed Jem into the far stall and we locked the door behind us.

She pulled down the change table, set her backpack on it, and pulled out a thermos and a Popsicle stick. She wriggled into a pair of latex gloves.

"Where'd you get those?"

Jem shrugged. "My mom uses them for when she colours her hair.

"Package?" she said in a whisper. She held her hand out to me as if she were a doctor who had just asked for a scalpel.

"What are you going to do?" I whispered back.

"I'm going to steam the package open so we can take a look inside."

I gave her the package. "Are you sure you know what you're doing?"

She nodded. "I googled it."

"What if you tear it?"

"Will you relax?" She looked up at me, put a hand on my shoulder, and said, "I've seen a million episodes of *Border Security*, besides. I know how it's done."

She unscrewed the thermos lid and steam wafted out from it.

"What's that?"

"Boiling water." She held the seal of the large, brown envelope over the thermos opening for a ten-count, then moved it slightly over to steam the next inch or two. When she was done, she placed it onto the change table, took the Popsicle stick, and slid it under the flap, gently nudging it as she went.

I'd never have thought it possible, but she managed to get the flap open without tearing it, and only minor puckering.

"Stand back," she said. "I'm going to turn it over."

"Why should I stand back? I want to see what's inside."

"You don't want to inhale it if it's anthrax or something."

"What about you?"

She looked at me sideways, as if pondering what I'd just said. "Right," she said, and pulled her t-shirt collar up and over her mouth and nose; I did the same.

"Here goes nothing," she said and upended the package.

A CD jewel case fell out along with a series of letter-sized papers, but no white powder, no wires, nothing even close to insidious. Up until that moment, I hadn't realized I'd been holding my breath. After we took stock of the contents of the envelope, a rush of air escaped from between my lips all on its own.

"Nothing."

"Don't sound so disappointed," I told her. I pulled my phone from my pocket to check the time. "Can we seal it back up and deliver it so we can get out of here?"

Jem nodded, slowly, as if in a daze, and I could tell she was disappointed. She'd never met Cain, so it couldn't be chalked up to a clash of personality, but I could tell she didn't like him. Maybe it was because we were so close before I'd met him. You know, I was new to the school, I came from a sheltered background, I had no friends, and Jem's history was similar to mine. We grew close quickly, probably because neither one of us had anyone else in our lives.

I hadn't been ignoring Jem—if she felt that way I was sorry, because it wasn't my intention. But I wasn't about to give Cain up and the way he made me feel to be alone with Jem.

Jem fished through her backpack and brought out a small, plastic package of glue tape, which she used to reseal the flap. "Good as new," she said.

I took the package from her and inspected it. It was *almost* good as new, if you ignored some of the pucker beneath the seal of the flap. "There's some pucker," I told her.

"Here," she said. She plucked the envelope from my hands, put it back on the change table, stuck her fingers into the open thermos, and wiped them across the flap to a point midway down the envelope.

"What are you doing?" I said, but it was too late to stop her.

She spun around to grab a wad of toilet paper, which she used to wipe off the excess water. When she was done, she tossed the paper into the toilet and handed the package back to me.

"It's still puckered," I said, after a full inspection.

"Yeah, but at least now it's not only on the flap."

I didn't know whether to hug her for covering for me or punch her in the face for making it worse, but time was ticking away. "Wait for me in the lobby," I told her, and went to deliver the package.

CHAPTER TWENTY

Cain and I took the subway to Queen Station and then a streetcar eastbound to the Beach Village. When we got off, he took me by the hand and led me through Kew Gardens Park toward the actual beach on the shore of Lake Ontario. The grounds of Kew Gardens were a lush, verdant green. We walked past a playground, rampant with kids and babies still in strollers, their parents or nannies nearby. When, at last, we reached the water, a wide, wooden boardwalk formed a barrier between grass and sand. Rollerbladers whizzed by us, as did people on bikes, skateboards, or jogging on foot. There were plenty of people walking, as well, strolling at the city's edge, taking advantage of the beautiful day.

"Come on," Cain said, as he took my hand. "The plan is to walk until we're tired, see if we can't find an ice cream vendor or something, and then keep walking until we stop for lunch."

"Sounds like a plan," I said, beaming. It was a Saturday, the first one since the incident that I had been allowed to go out on a weekend. I'd told Dad I was going to the Eaton Centre with Jem, only this time, Jem was in on the deception, so it'd be okay. As an added measure, I turned off the GPS tracker on my phone and told Jem to do the same, just in case

Dad thought he'd check up on me and then enlist her father to check up on her.

After we'd walked a while, Cain found a guy selling frozen treats from an ice cream cart, and we bought a couple of Drumsticks. There was this outcropping of boulders on the water's edge and we sat there to have our snack.

"If you're hot, you can dip your feet in the water, you know," Cain told me.

I shook my head. "No thanks."

"Check out the sign." He pointed with his Drumstick. "It says it's safe to go into the water today."

Summers in Toronto, lately, have been super-hot, like, approaching 40 degrees hot, and lots of news outlets regularly announce the opening of what the government calls "Cooling Stations". Cooling Stations include everything from pools open to the public to air conditioned community centres and open and safe beaches. All it takes is for a single rainstorm to stir all of the crud on the lake's floor into the water and the beaches could be closed to swimmers for days. Just because the sign said it was safe, just because the surface water tested safe, didn't mean the stuff I'd be stepping in was safe if I were to wade in.

I tell this to Cain and say, "You of all people should know that."

He nodded. "I do. And just for the record, I didn't *say* you should wade in, I only suggested you *might* dip your feet in to cool down, as in, use the part that's been tested as safe."

"Seriously?"

Cain only chuckled.

When he was done his ice cream, he picked up a stone and threw it into the water.

"That's not how you skip a stone," I said.

"I wasn't trying to skip it."

I looked up at him, pasted on a devilish smile, and said, "You don't know how to skip a stone, do you."

"Of course I do," he said confidently, but he couldn't hide the hint of blush that grew on his cheeks. "Everyone knows how to skip a stone."

"Prove it."

"Okay," he said. He left the outcropping of boulders we were on to search for a flat stone. When he found one, he came back to me, stood sideways on the rock closest to the water, and threw it as he might throw a Frisbee. The rock travelled a few metres before thunking into the water.

"Maybe a jump rope's more your speed," I said. "You *do* know how to skip a rope?"

He curled his lips into a mock scowl. "Okay, smarty. Put your money where your mouth is." He handed me a smooth, flat stone.

"Maybe I will," I said. I popped the tip of my cone into my mouth, stood up, and brushed the sand from my shorts. "Watch and learn," I said. I made a show of my wind-up and my pitch. The stone travelled about the same distance as did his, skimmed the water, went another few centimetres, and then fell into the water with a muted blurt.

"Yes!" I said, doing a fist pump.

"One skip? That's the best you can do?"

"One is better than none."

"So," he said, hooking his arm around my waist and pulling me close, "one kiss would be better than none?"

"Uh-huh," I said. I meant for it to be defiant, proud, victorious. Instead, it came out as more of a whisper.

"To the spoils go the victor," he said, and kissed me on the lips. It was tender, dry, and lasted no more than a second or two, but I thanked my lucky stars he had his arms around me to hold me up because it was enough to turn my legs to molten wax.

We shared a look after we broke the kiss. Cain had been the first to break the kiss and the gaze that followed. He crossed his legs at the ankles and sat back down on the largest boulder, cross-legged. When he pulled me down, it was to sit in his lap.

"I have to go away for a bit," he said.

My heart began to skitter before I was able to form my next word. "What?"

"Jo-Jo has a job for me. Something about a demonstration happening at Queen's Park. In Ottawa."

"Can't he send someone else?" I turned my head, craning my neck as I tried to see the expression on his face. Luckily, he craned his neck as well, stretching it to meet me halfway.

"I'm his recruiter, remember? He needs me to recruit."

"Recruit whom?"

Cain shrugged. "Something about marijuana legalization."

"You're going to Ottawa to smoke pot?" I tried to get up from his lap but he tightened his grip on me.

"I'm going to check out who's there. Gauge their opinions. Make some contacts."

"Contacts for what?"

He shrugged again. "Jo-Jo has a plan. He'll let me know when we get there, I suppose."

I thought for a moment. "Who's we?"

"Me and Joj."

"Can I go, too?"

"What would you tell your dad?"

I shook my head. "I'll think of something."

Cain squeezed me and kissed the crook of my neck, making me shiver in spite of the heat of the day, in spite of the fact that the warmth of his body was making my legs sweat where my skin made contact with his. "As much as I'd love for you to come, you're a minor. I don't think it's the best place for you, seeing as we expect to come away with a contact high."

"And you're okay with that?"

"It's a sacrifice. For the greater good."

I exhaled. He was going to leave me, and there was nothing I could do to stop it. My eyes burned with tears at the mere thought of it. How would I react when it finally happened?

"For how long?" I asked.

Cain shrugged. "Don't know. As long as Joj needs me to be there."

I broke his hold on me to twist around so I could see his face. I wanted to see the same anguish in his eyes that I felt in my heart and soul. "How *long*, Cain?"

"At least a week," he said. He looked away from me when he spoke, as if the truth of our separation was too much for him to bear. I *hoped* our separation would be too much for him to bear, at any rate. It was already too much for me, and he was still sitting right in front of me.

"Maybe more," he admitted.

"When?" I demanded.

Cain stared out over the water, squinting against the reflection of the sun on its surface.

I put my finger under his chin and used it to move his face until our eyes made contact. The bristle of his beard pricked my fingers, like an array of teeny tiny pins. "*When*, Cain?"

"Tomorrow." His voice cracked when he spoke.

"Well," I said, standing up. "So nice of you to tell me before you left."

"It's not like that, Jude," he said, practically whining.

"Then why don't you tell me what it *is* like?"

Cain stood up beside me. He placed his hands on my shoulders and twisted my upper body to face him. "Jo-Jo asked me to go last week. I begged him not to send me. I told him I didn't want to go, that I didn't want to leave you. He said he'd try to send someone else, but in the end he couldn't. I just found out, myself.

"Look, I don't want to go any more than you want me to go—"

"So tell him no."

"I can't. He's like my father—"

"You have no problem with me going against *my* father's wishes—"

"What's that supposed to mean? If you recall, I was the one who told you not to lie to him after the last time."

"Don't go," I said, emphatically. It was an order, not a request.

"I *have* to go. I owe him."

"What kind of parent makes his child owe him for raising him?"

"You're twisting my words." He tried to pull me toward him for a hug, but I resisted. "I have this...arrangement with him. We do things for each other. If he needs me to go then I have to go, no questions asked."

"It's a stupid arrangement," I said. I crossed my arms over my chest. It felt like pouting, but I didn't care.

Cain smiled, released a breathy chuckle, and tried to hold me again. At first, I resisted, but then he tried even harder. Rather than turn it into a full-out struggle, I let him take me into his arms. I didn't know who I hated more at that point—Jo-Jo for taking Cain from me, or Cain for letting him.

"It is," Cain said. "It's a stupid, stupid arrangement."

We stood there for a few moments, enjoying the heat of our embrace, the warmth of each other's breath on our skin. When at last Cain broke the embrace, he said, "There's more."

"Is it good news, or bad?"

"Good, I think."

"I could stand a bit of good news right now."

"Jo-Jo has one last job for you to do before he goes."

"*Last* job? But...you said you'd be back."

"We will. He'll have more work for you once we return."

"But you *will* return, right?"

"Of course, I will," he said. He flashed his mesmerizingly gorgeous smile, and I almost believed what he said to be true.

"Promise?"

"I promise."

I nodded. "What's the job?"

"A delivery. To the Financial District. After school tomorrow. John will pick you up and take you to the subway. He'll have the package with him."

"Same as before?"

Cain gave an exaggerated nod. "Same as before. Get there before closing, deliver the package, and go home.

"Can you do that? For me?"

"Have I ever let you down before?" I threw my arms around his shoulders and squeezed, but he took me by the wrists, forcing my arms away from his neck and down to my side.

"I mean it," he said. "No dawdling. No stopping, not even for a drink, not until after you get back to Finch."

"O...kay?" I said it just like that, split into two words with a question mark at the end. It was weird. Since when did he care if I took an extra five or so minutes to get a slushy drink somewhere?

"I just..." He looked at me as if he were frustrated with me. He frowned. "I just don't want your dad to worry. You said you needed to get home before he did."

"Okay," I said, more emphatically.

"I mean it. Promise me, Jude."

"*Okay.*"

"I need you to say it. Say you promise me no dawdling after the delivery."

"I promise," I said. "Straight home after the delivery."

CHAPTER TWENTY-ONE

John looked vaguely familiar when he approached me outside of school the next day, like I'd seen him hanging at Jo-Jo's or something. He put a hand on the small of my back as he led me across the street to his car, which was sort of weird because he was in such close proximity and I hardly knew him, if at all. He held the passenger's side door open for me and closed it behind me once I'd gotten in.

We drove to the subway in silence, and I mean silence—he didn't even have the radio on. I looked over at him a few times, too, but he was too focussed on the road to even notice.

When we pulled into the Kiss and Ride at Finch Station he circled around until he found a parking space. He turned the engine off after he'd parked, reached into the back seat, and gave me a small box, wrapped in brown paper. "As usual, Judith: get in, get out, draw no undue attention."

"This isn't my first rodeo, you know."

He looked at me as if I'd spoken in Chinese or something.

"I know the drill. Cain trained me well."

"No loitering, either."

I nodded. "Cain told me that, too."

There was another moment of silence between us, even more awkward than on the drive down there, if that were even possible. "Have you heard from Cain? Did he make it to Ottawa okay?" I said, hopeful for news.

"Is that where he's gone to?"

"He's supposed to have gone with Jo-Jo."

John shrugged. "Jo-Jo compartmentalizes. If you're a courier, you courier. If you're a recruiter, you recruit. The left hand never knows what the right's doing unless it needs to know to do its job."

"That's kind of weird, don't you think?"

John shrugged again and said, "Mine's not to reason why."

I knew that passage—it was from Tennyson's *The Charge of the Light Brigade*: "Theirs not to reason why, theirs but to do or die"—and I didn't like it, not one bit, especially not the part about doing and dying.

"Here," John said. He handed me an envelope. I knew what was inside: payment. For a job well done.

"There's a note in there, too. In case you have to reach one of us. After."

I turned to look at him, feeling the tension in my forehead grow. "After what?"

"After the job. You know, 'cause Cain won't be around for a while."

I didn't mention that I had his phone number. I knew where Jo-Jo lived, besides.

"Take care, Judith," John said. I took that as my cue to leave, so I did. Standing on the curb outside of the rotunda, I considered that my experience with the guy had been a bit surreal, but it was the first time he'd ever dropped me off, the first time anyone other than Cain had couriered me to the station. The first time Cain hadn't couriered the courier.

Was that was I was? A courier?

Why did this time seem so different than the others? Was it because Cain hadn't seen me off?

Why was John acting so weird in the car? Why was there no attempt to even make casual conversation?

Maybe John was lacking in social skills. Maybe he had the same kind of social anxiety I did when it came to strangers. I'd have to try to engage him a bit more next time to figure it out, I guess.

John honked two short blasts at me as he passed on his way out of the parking lot. I sighed, folded the envelope, stuffed it into my purse, and slid the package into my backpack.

In the Financial District, I found the building, went in, and went directly to the fourth floor. There was a large counter opposite the elevators, but there was no one sitting behind it. I waited for a few minutes, but the secretary never came.

The label on the package read "Suite 412". Would it be weird for me to try to find the office on my own?

"Hello?" I asked. People walked back and forth behind me, from one side of the floor to the other, but it was as if I were invisible. Not a single one of them asked me if I was in the right place, or whom I wanted to see.

I took a closer look at the top of the counter, hoping to find a bell or something, but there was nothing on it outside of a vase of daffodils and a box of Kleenex.

"Hello?" I said again. "Package delivery."

I waited for a hundred count. Still no one, so I decided to find Suite 412 on my own.

There was a central hub of enclosed offices in the middle of the floor, just beyond the waiting area, and a series of cubicles in between. Suite 412 was one of the centre offices.

I knocked on the door but there was no answer. Someone walked by me and I said, "Excuse me?" but she continued to walk as if I weren't there.

"I have a delivery?" I said to a man wearing a dark suit and blood-red tie, but he walked by me, too.

In the end, I decided to leave the package just inside the open office door, and head home.

CHAPTER TWENTY-TWO

The next day, around nine-thirty am, Mr. Carey, our vice principal, came to the door of our classroom and asked to speak with our teacher in the hall. Mr. Carey was a regular fixture in most classrooms. Unlike the other VP or the principal, he was known to drop into class and watch—though whether it was us or the teacher he was observing was still unclear. Some days, horror of horrors, he approached students and asked them weird questions, like "What were we doing?" and worse, "Why were we doing it?" Luckily, the teacher always had that information on the board, so we could surreptitiously glance over at it and let him know, but I lived in fear of the day he would ask me and I couldn't answer. I mean, this wasn't like admitting to your teacher you hadn't done your homework— that was bad enough because you had to see her every day and spend the rest of the semester making it up to her—this was even worse. As vice principal, he was like the vice president of the school or something, and then you had to spend every day of the next few years ducking him in the hallway so you wouldn't feel embarrassed for giving him that one stupid answer that one time he chose you to ask one of his weird questions.

The whole situation was weird, too, because outside of the odd nod or smile, the two of them never acknowledged each other and rarely ever spoke. It was almost like the teacher knew he'd be coming in and she was okay with him just lurking like that. If I was so stressed sitting at my desk doing my work or listening to her speak, imagine how she felt.

They stood in the doorway for a few minutes, him talking, her nodding, or asking a question, but mostly it was him talking. The buzz in the classroom grew. What was going on? Had someone been hurt? A few kids took a quick headcount of the students present and the students absent and wondered who was away and if it was about one of them. Some of them grew as pensive as the teacher, and I remember thinking: I wonder if they think it's about them? Maybe someone was going to be suspended or expelled. Maybe someone in their family had died and they were about to get the news.

When they parted and the teacher returned, she looked solemn and was particularly quiet. She made a bee-line to the computers at the back of the classroom, jiggled the mouse, and signed in without speaking to anyone. As she waited for her profile to load, she said, "Ladies and gentlemen." She always began her announcements like that. It was kind of cool. I've had teachers address us as "guys", "children", "boys and girls", and even "turkeys", but none of them like that, like we were peers. It made us feel like if we were worthy of that kind of respect from her, she was worthy of our attention.

"I've just been informed there's been a bombing downtown. Mr. Carey says they don't know if it's a terrorist attack or simply due to a gas leak, but he's asked that we monitor the situation in our classrooms. The admin's cancelled period two so we can watch from here." She logged into CP24, the

144

local, all-news channel. Reception was choppy, probably due to the fact that everyone in the school was trying to access either that site, CNN, or something like it, and that, city-wide, people were probably going to CP24, as it was most people's go-to station for quick news-bites (it certainly was my dad's).

She turned on the overhead projector and we watched as the story unfolded.

The explosion happened shortly after nine am, so we were watching the aftermath of the disaster almost as it unfolded. So far there were three people dead and nine injured. They showed the building, still in flames, and the firemen trying to put it out. I watched the footage, looking for any landmarks that would help me to know where, exactly, downtown it was.

The Eaton Centre was a good target, plenty of people, shopping, working, and offices nearby.

Union Station was another. Though it would have been the tail-end of rush hour at the time and most people would already be at work, it still would have been bustling, as it was the main transportation hub in the city.

Then there was the CN Tower. Imagine the devastation in the city of one of the world's tallest buildings collapsed. How far might the debris field go?

Any of the universities would also make a suitable target. So would the so-called "Hospital Row", the section of University Avenue with wall-to-wall hospitals on either side, Queen's Park, and the government offices there, or the Royal Ontario Museum.

The image on the screen shifted from the flaming, smoking building, back to the studio reporter who said, "If you're just joining us, we're covering an apparent terrorist attack that happened

145

at precisely 9:15 this morning in the Financial District—"

An explosion in the Financial District.

I was just there yesterday, delivering my package. Boy, was I lucky! Had I been asked to deliver it this morning, instead, I might have been there when—

I delivered a package just yesterday. Near closing time. In the Financial District.

Where in the Financial District? my brain screamed at me. Why didn't they give us an address?

Though they never did say the address, a picture of the building before the disaster was plastered across the screen as the reporter continued to speak about casualties in voice-over.

It was the same building to which I'd delivered my package.

When I was at the reception desk, no one was there to stop me from wandering into the office space. Everyone was busy, hustling to and fro. Too busy to notice a random box in brown paper wrapping sitting just inside a random office.

What if the person had already gone home for the evening?

What if he had come in the next morning, noticed the package, and brought it further into his office.

What if it sat there on his desk for about fifteen minutes, unopened, undiscovered, until...

No. That was impossible.

Jo-Jo did desk-top publishing, for heaven's sake! He was an artist, a businessman.

Jo-Jo would never—

Cain would never!

It suddenly became hard to breathe. Black spots gathered in my peripheral vision and then spread. Try as I might, I couldn't take any air into my lungs. It was like when you cried and I mean,

146

hard, like when you finally realize your mom is dead and you'll never see her again, never feel her touch, never hear her voice. When you cry with the pain of an infant who thinks the hunger she's feeling is the end of her world, and she exhales and it's like a switch has been flipped and even though she wants to inhale, she no longer can, because her body won't let her flip that switch back, and she just sits there, tears streaming down her cheeks, mouth open wide, cheeks turning blue because she can't breathe, like, she physically can't breathe. That's exactly what I felt at that moment.

"Jude?" Jem said to me. "Are you okay?"

I wanted to answer her, No, I'm not okay. Can't you see that I can't breathe? Don't you know that you were right all along? That even if the envelope didn't contain Anthrax that one time, it contained something even worse this time? That I trusted Jo-Jo, I trusted Cain, and the two of them have turned me into a terrorist? Into a murderer? Into a *multiple* murderer?

Instead, I just sit there, mouth open, lungs empty, my brain refusing to flip the switch from exhale to inhale, the black spots slowly covering my entire field of vision, like dark ooze being poured into a container, slogging back and forth until it settles in front of me, and I start to feel light headed.

"Miss Granger?" Jem said.

"Miss Granger?" she repeated even louder. "Help! Jude's not breathing!"

She rushed over, knelt down in front of me, put her hands on my shoulders, and said, "Judith? Honey, you have to breathe."

Duh! I wanted to say, but I couldn't because my body wouldn't let me get enough air in order to speak.

"Judith?" She looked me in the eyes and then turned to Jem and told her to go to the phone and dial the emergency office number.

Instead, Jem started to rub my back. Miss Granger called Jem's name again, but Jem stayed behind me. Someone else must have gotten up to make the phone call because I heard her talking in the background. Part of my brain was listening to the girl, frantic on the phone, part of my brain was registering Jem's hand on my back and Miss Granger's hands on my shoulders and the other part of my brain was yelling at the rest of my brain to breathe. Just when I felt my eyes closing and like I was going to fall from my chair, Jem hit my back. It felt as if I'd been kicked by a mule, but it did the trick, and I gulped in this huge breath of air. The blackness subsided. I felt kind of nauseated, but soon that started to subside as well.

I took a few more gulps of air and noticed Mr. Carey was back, only this time, he was pushing a wheelchair.

CHAPTER TWENTY-THREE

T he trip to the office was mortifying. My class is on the far end of the building, and the elevator is somewhere in the middle. I told Mr. Carey I really was fine and that I could go back to class. When he didn't listen, I begged, "At least let me walk to the office."

"Sorry," he said. "Protocol."

He wanted to talk the whole way, asking me things like if I was okay, or what had happened, or if I was prone to anxiety attacks.

I answered him plainly: yes, I was okay; I don't know what happened; no, I wasn't prone to attacks.

"Can I just..." I finally said. "I'm feeling like I might throw up, and I just want to sit quietly." It was a lie, but he got the message and clammed up.

In the office, he asked if I was okay to get up from the chair and then told me to lie down.

"I'm fine, really," I said.

He looked at me sternly through the glare of his glasses.

"What if I just sit?"

"It's a start," he said.

He folded up the wheelchair and started to leave the room.

"What happens now?" I asked.

"We call your parents to come and get you so you can go home and rest."

"Can't I just go home on my own?"

He shook his head. "There's something called liability involved. Do you know what liability means?"

I nodded my head; I watch *Judge Judy*.

"It's just..." I paused, trying to find the right words. "If he has to leave work he won't get paid for the time he's missed, and money's already tight as it is. I don't want to be the reason why he comes up short this week."

"I'll see what I can do," he said with a smile.

The whole time he was gone, the image from the news broadcast played over and over again in my head. People were hurt—nine so far—that was bad enough, but there was a death toll of three, as well. I thought back to the footage I'd seen of the 9/11 attacks, and then the ones of the Boston Marathon. People had been maimed. They'd lost limbs. Families had lost children and parents.

I couldn't bear the notion that this time that would be on me.

The air grew thick again. It felt saturated with water, or my lungs felt full of water and the air was normal. In any case, it was getting harder and harder to breathe the more I thought about it.

I told myself that it wasn't on me, that it was on that guy John, the one who had given me the package. It was on Jo-Jo for assigning the package to me. It was on Cain for recruiting me, for getting me caught up in this mess in the first place.

The black spots returned to my peripheral vision about the same time as Mr. Carey.

"Whoa, whoa, whoa," he said. "How's it going, Judith?"

How do you think it's going? I wanted to say, but I couldn't get enough air into my lungs to back a sound other than a repeating wheeze.

"Lie back," he told me, and this time I did.

When I opened my eyes, his face was practically next to mine, his blue eyes amplified by the lenses of his glasses. "Try counting backward from ten."

I shook my head. The blackness threatened to capture my entire field of vision, and I started to panic. I wanted to stand up, but he put his hands on my shoulders and held me down, which had the same effect as holding a drowning man under water. As far as I was concerned—it made it worse. I mean, seriously, did this guy even have any first aid training?

"I need to sit up!" I said and practically pushed him out of the way. I leaned forward, resting my elbows on my legs and hanging my head near my knees.

"Better?" I could still feel his hand on my shoulder.

"Better."

"Your dad's managed to change his lunch so he can come and get you."

I nodded. It was all I could think of to do.

Dad came for me just before one. The VP brought him right back into the sick room to see me. By then, I'd managed to calm down, and was able to lie down, but only if I concentrated on Fall Out Boys' song lyrics. Anything else, even if it were just the inkling of what was unfolding downtown, and it was likely to set off another attack.

"You okay, sweetie?" Dad asked.

"Fine," I said, getting up. I picked my backpack up and slung a strap over my shoulder. "Can we go now?"

Driving home in the car, Dad said, "I understand it was bad."

"Huh? Yeah. Pretty much." I was trying to distract myself with the scenery, waiting until I could go home, crawl under the blankets, blare my music, and contact Cain.

Cain. My phone was buried in my backpack the whole time I was in the sick room. Half of the time I couldn't move for fear I might keel over, the other half of the time I didn't want to draw attention to myself. I mean, what if I really was responsible for what had happened? What might happen then? Would the school call the police? Would they arrest me? Take me out in handcuffs?

"I texted Jem," Dad says. "She says she's happy to come over after school to keep you company, if you like."

It was probably my fault that Dad and Jem had each other in their contacts list. I mean, had I not disappeared to be with Cain that weekend, they might never have talked. Ever.

"I want to be alone."

Dad looked over at me. "What happened, Jude?" He never called me Jude, at least, not until I'd met Jem and she started doing it.

"I don't know," I said. "Maybe I'm coming down with something."

"Maybe you should see your doctor—"

"I said I was fine. Can you please just drop it?" I didn't mean to snap at him, but I was frustrated, scared, freaking out, and it just came out that way.

"Promise me that if it happens again—"

"If it happens again I'll go see my doctor."

He chanced another glance.

"Happy now?"

"Not happy, no. Worried."

"Tell Jem I said no thank you."

"Why don't *you* text her? She's worried, too."

"You invited her, you cancel her."

"Fine."

We drove in silence the rest of the way home. When he dropped me off, he pulled into the driveway and I got out without saying another word. I closed the door behind me, disappointed that it didn't make a louder noise as it shut.

CHAPTER TWENTY-FOUR

Once inside the house, I ran up to my room and threw myself onto the bed, doing a face-plant into the pillow.

What have I done?

Nothing. You've done nothing. You had no way of knowing what was in that package.

Jem knew. That's why she had me open the last delivery.

But the last delivery was clean. There was no way to know this would be the one, that I...

I was a murderer!

The last thought hit me hard, and my crying turned to sobbing.

Three people dead at last count.

I was going to jail!

My sobs turned to wails, and I was glad that I was alone.

I grabbed my plush, stuffed Belle doll and held her. Mom had taken me out to buy Belle as a reward for going potty when I was about two and a half. She'd said I could have any toy I wanted, and I'd chosen her. She was so pretty, sitting in her yellow box adorned with purple flowers that matched the ones on her dress. Her hair was fuzzy and plush, too, her yellow dress, gauzy. She had perfectly bowed, puckered, purple lips and rosy

154

cheeks, and I knew right away she was what I'd wanted. She's always been with me, first when I was younger because I loved her, then when I got older because she held fond memories of my childhood. When Mom died, I'd started sleeping with her again, because she made me feel closer to her. When I was younger, Mom had always reminded me about Belle, and that she'd bought her as a potty toy, and that I should be proud that I was a big girl. When she was gone, it became sort of a talisman for her love, a touchstone for her pride.

As I wailed, I hugged Belle tightly in my arms and rocked myself for comfort.

At some point, I must've fallen asleep, because next thing I knew, it was evening. I got up to see if Dad's car was in the drive. It wasn't, but that didn't mean he wasn't home. I didn't want to leave my room to call him because I didn't want to talk to him. He'd want to know why I'd had a panic attack, and I could just imagine how that conversation would go:

"Why'd you have a panic attack, dear?" Dad would ask in a concerned tone. His eyebrows would furrow together, and the worry lines would form.

"Well, you see, Dad," I would say, "I'm still seeing Cain, even though you said not to."

"Well, I can't say I'm not disappointed, Judith," Dad would answer.

"And I've been working as a courier for this guy who's sort of like Cain's surrogate father, and you know the bomb that went off in the Financial District? I delivered it."

I'd want him to take me in his arms, smooth my hair and rub my back like he did when I was a kid and had fallen and scraped my knee or something. "It's okay, Judith. We'll figure something out," is what I'd want him to say.

Judging the way he'd reacted that time I went to the conservation area, my fantasy conversation most likely couldn't be further from what would unfold in reality.

Dad would go ballistic and rightly so. His world was about to fall apart. First, he'd lost Mom, now he was going to lose me. Trust me, I know. My world had also fallen apart at that point, and it only promised to get worse.

I needed to speak with Cain.

My phone was still at the bottom of my backpack, so I dug it out.

Sixteen text messages.

Six from Jem.

Ten from Dad.

Just then the house phone started to ring. When the machine picked up, I heard Dad's voice say, "Judith? Are you there?" There was a long pause and then he said, "Judith, please pick up." Another pause. "It's Dad."

Duh.

"I'm...I'm worried about you, sweetheart...Just...please call to let me know you're okay." He hung up and the machine beeped.

How many times had he called when I was asleep? How many of those messages might I find if I went downstairs to check the number on the machine? How long before he was worried enough to leave work and come home to check up on me?

Then I remembered: Cain. I went to get my phone to contact Cain.

Why were none of my messages from him?

I opened my messaging app and typed, *WTF, Cain?*

My finger hovered over the little paper airplane icon. Should I send; shouldn't I send?

I erased the message and typed, *Cain? U there?* instead.

The response was almost instantaneous: *Error. Invalid number. Please resend text message using a valid 10-digit number.*

That couldn't be right.

I went into my contacts list, clicked on his entry, and speed-dialed his number.

The message was immediate: "The number you have dialed is not a working number. Please try again using a valid 10-digit number."

The number *was* valid. The day before.

The recording repeated as I slowly lowered the phone from my ear.

Stunned, I disconnected and dialed the number using brute force and from my dad's land line, with the same results.

Why would Cain disconnect his number and not tell me?

There was only one thing I could do—I needed to go to Jo-Jo's and track him down. I turned my purse upside down, but couldn't find my bus pass. I also didn't have any change.

On the hunt for bus fare, I practically ransacked my room, my dad's room, and every other living space in the house. I found a loony, a few quarters, and a dime—hardly enough for a one-way fare, let alone the return.

I needed to find my bus pass, so I went back to my room.

My backpack was sitting on the floor in the corner, slumped against the wall. When I saw it, I realized I hadn't checked there yet. I upturned the backpack, to no avail. Though I didn't find my pass, I did find the envelope that guy, John, had given me when he'd dropped me off at the station. Inside were a few hundred dollars in hundred-dollar bills.

My pay off.

Blood money.

Did that make me a hit man? Or, rather, a hit woman?

A hundred-dollar bill wouldn't get me onto the bus, so I dumped the contents of the envelope over, looking for I knew not what, in case there was something else inside.

A small piece of newsprint fluttered out of the envelope, delicate as a feather, and settled on the pile of bills on my floor. On the newsprint was an ad from *The Toronto Star* that read:

```
RECRUITS WANTED
Apply in person.
```

It was a sign. From Cain. Was that how I was supposed to reach him?

My train of thought was interrupted when the doorbell rang. A full five minutes after that, it rang again. And then again, five minutes after that. Then whoever was there began to knock. I got up to look out of my window and recognized Jem's father's car in the driveway.

It figures Dad would send her instead of coming to check on me himself. I'm surprised he hadn't given her a key.

I left my room to sit at the top of the stairs. There's a huge, stained glass window in our front door, and through it, I watched as Jem and another figure, probably her dad, just stood there, trying to figure out what to do next. At one point, Jem put her nose right up against the glass and used her hands like blinders, one on each side of her face, to try to see inside.

Sitting at the top of the stairs, hugging my knees, a part of me wanted to leap down the steps, open the door, go to her, hug her, and tell her everything. But a part of me knew that what I did wasn't so easily forgiven. And the last thing I wanted at that point in time was an I told you so, so I watched and waited.

When she couldn't see anything, she turned to her father and they spoke, but what they said was too muffled for me to make out the words. Jem took out her phone and made a call—I can only assume it was to my dad—and then she left. When I was sure she was gone, I went back to bed and cried myself to sleep.

CHAPTER TWENTY-FIVE

I awoke to Dad calling my name. The room had grown appreciably darker at that time, and my father appeared as a shadow figure in the doorway, backlit by the light from the hall. I didn't say anything at first, so he repeated my name again.

"What?" I said, rather angrily.

He let out a long hiss of air. "You're still alive. That's good."

"Is that supposed to be a joke or something?"

He was silent for a moment and then said, "I brought home pizza. Anchovies and red onions, just the way you like it. I thought you could use some comfort food."

"I'm not hungry."

"Look, Judith," he said. He came the rest of the way into my room and sat down at the foot of my bed. "I don't know what's going on with you, what happened today, but I want you to know I'm here for you. In case you want to, you know, talk. I thought we could do it over dinner. I picked up extra dipping sauce, and those bar-b-que, meat-flavoured chips you like, too."

"Not hungry."

"Okay," he said. He squeezed my foot through the blanket. "Just so you know: when you're ready, I'm here."

Dad turned the television off in his room around 9:30. Sometimes he'll sit up with me if there's a movie on or something, but most of the time he's in his room before nine and asleep in front of the TV before ten. Most nights I go in there and turn it off before I turn in around 11. Dad's lonely. He works long hours and comes home to an empty house with a daughter he doesn't understand, an empty bed, and no one to talk to about the heavy stuff. I hoped he'd go see a therapist, sometime soon. I was sure he would need it, especially after my recent crap hit the fan.

I waited a whole half hour afterward, just to be sure. Usually, he's already asleep when the TV goes off, but I needed to know he wouldn't catch me when I snuck downstairs to use the family computer around ten. Our house is kind of old. Built in the eighties, it has minor foundation problems because it's settled, big-time. Though it's not noticeable to the naked eye, the whole house slumps to one side. If you spill some water on the counter, it's only a matter of time before it finds its way to the far side of the counter and spills down onto the floor. If you drop a pencil on the floor near the sink, it'll start to roll, all on its own, until it gets lost under the fridge in a matter of seconds.

As I descended the stairs I thought of that story Scout tells about the Finch's Landing house in *To Kill A Mockingbird*, the one where the Finch ancestor had designed the house so that the only entrance and exit to his daughters' rooms were through a staircase in his bedroom, and wondered if Dad, for all his worrying, ever thought to redesign the house to be the same. In any case, practically every stair and floorboard in the house creaked when you stepped on it and I was worried Dad would hear me on the way down. I travelled in darkness, not wanting to chance the lights waking him, in case the floorboards didn't.

Once his computer booted, I went to thestar.com and clicked over to the classifieds page, where I could put both a digital and print ad on at the same time, but I needed a credit card to do it. I was hoping I could use PayPal (I know Dad's email address, and his password is always the same— Mom's maiden name and the year of her birth), but there was no option for that. Luckily, I do have a credit card, one Dad made me swear I'd only use in case of an emergency. He'd given it to me after Mom had died, and told me to only use it if I were over a barrel. For months afterward, he reminded me that he got all of the bills, so he'd know if I were being irresponsible with it. He said it had a limit of fifty dollars, but that he'd up it if I proved I could manage it. I guess he was happy with how I'd used it in the past because the limit was up somewhere around two hundred dollars by then.

Trouble was, my card was in my wallet, which was in my backpack, which was all the way back up the squeaky staircase in my room. Dad's wallet, however, was in his jacket pocket, which he kept in the downstairs coat closet.

I crept up the basement stairs, leaving Dad's office light on so I wouldn't stumble, and opened the closet door. The zipper from one of my sweatshirts clinked against the back of the door.

Betrayed by an item of my own clothing!

Frozen, unable to move, unable to breathe for a good thirty seconds, I waited for Dad to peek his head over the second floor banister and ask me what I thought I was doing, creeping around the house in the middle of the night.

Luckily, that confrontation never came about.

When I was sure Dad was still upstairs, fast asleep, I slid his wallet from his jacket's breast pocket and tip-toed back downstairs.

Before I could place an ad, I had to create an account, which I did—in Dad's name but using my email address—verified the account when the email came, and placed an ad that said:

```
RECRUITS WANTED
Apply in person.
```

I followed this up with the words:

```
Food Court, pm
```

hoping Cain would make the connection to the place we'd first met and know it was from me. I decided to run the ad for a full week, in case he didn't check it every day. It cost a pretty penny, but since it was near the beginning of the month, I felt sure this had bought me a little time, as it would be a few weeks before Dad would be billed for the ad, and as they say in the old gangster movies, the jig would be up.

I shut the computer down, put Dad's wallet back into his pocket, and snuck back upstairs to my room. When I was under the blankets, I took hold of Belle and hugged her tightly.

"Mom?" I whispered. "Why did you have to go so soon?" My eyes burned as tears threatened to come. I often talk to my mom when I'm alone. Actually, I talk to myself but pretended it's to my mom. I mean, I never thought my mom was actually listening. I think I just find it easier to work through problems if I speak the words rather than think them, but I feel stupid talking to myself, so I pretend I'm actually talking to her, like she's sitting in the room with me, nodding her head, saying "uh-huh" every so often to show me she's still listening.

163

"I need you, Mom." I swallowed some of the bile collecting at the back of my throat. "I've gotten myself into trouble and I don't know what to do." The first of many tears to come fell from my eye to my cheek. "I met this boy. His name is Cain. He is the most beautiful thing I've ever seen. He's older, but he's so kind and gentle and he makes me feel almost as beautiful as I think he is.

"Dad's struggling. He misses you, and he thinks he needs to work all of this overtime to make ends meet, but I think it's because he doesn't like to come home and not be able to share his work stories with you, like you guys used to. He's never here, and I'm lonely.

"I have Jem, my friend—you've never met her, either, but she's probably the closest I've ever been to another person, besides you and Dad, of course. And Cain. But that's not the same as having a parent here to look after you and make sure you're safe. That's what Cain does for me—makes me feel safe.

"I thought that if I had a job, Dad might be able to work a bit less, you know? So I went looking. To help him out. And that's when I met Cain. And he gave me a job, delivering these packages for his boss.

"Jem was worried, but I told her it was okay. We even opened up one of the packages and it was nothing but business cards and stationary, so I knew it was okay.

"His boss even pays me, and the people getting the deliveries give me tips, so the money's good, and I don't have to ask Dad for any anymore, but I think he's too busy to notice.

"When Dad found out about Cain, he went ballistic, because he's older than me, and I took off one day without Dad's permission, and he blamed Cain for it." Tears flowed freely down my face at that point, enough to wet the pillow beneath my head

164

(and probably Belle's head as well). My nose was running, and I was sniffling so hard I was practically snorting.

"He told me I couldn't see Cain anymore, but I didn't listen. I mean, Jem's my friend and all, but she can't make me feel the way Cain does: needed, wanted, loved. And Dad's at work all the time...

"When Cain's friend, that John guy, gave me the package to deliver instead of Cain himself, I should've known something was up, but I like the way Cain makes me feel, not sexually or anything like that—we've only ever held hands and kissed— but beautiful, like I matter, and I didn't want to disappoint him, so I went through with the delivery." A great, heaving sob took me by surprise, making it hard to breathe. I rode it through, like a surfer upon a great wave, until it dissipated.

"I didn't know this would happen, I mean, how *could* I know? I trusted him! I trusted him! I trusted...

"Anyway, now people are dead, some are dying, others are hurt or maimed for life, all because of me, because I was too stupid to question the situation, too stupid to question, period." This was followed by another wave of great, heaving sobs. The muscles around my heart contracted at one point and my lungs froze after a mondo exhalation of air. Just as I was sure I'd never breathe again, just as black spots formed in my periphery and grew to threaten my vision entirely, the muscles relaxed, and I was able to take in a titanic gulp of air.

"How can I live with myself knowing I'm a murderer?" I asked Mom once I was able. "I'll go to jail, for sure. How can I face Dad after this?" My lip trembled during the pause. "I only wanted to help. I only wanted it to be easier for him. Instead, I've made this mammoth mess!

"I need you, Mom. I want you to be here to tell me everything will be okay. I want to feel your lips and breath on my forehead as you hug me and make it better. I mean, I know this can't be made better, but...

"I miss you. I want *you*, and all I have instead is this stupid potty doll." Forgetting the time of night and that Dad was asleep not too far down the hall, I whipped Belle across the room. She hit the wall with a thud, rebounded, and landed on the floor like a brick. There were a few more minutes of sobbing and heaving before I went to retrieve her. I brought her back to bed, hugged her tightly in my arms, and just sat there, rocking.

I fell asleep at some point because I recall waking and feeling as if I weren't alone. I'd never believed in ghosts. Mom always told these stories about things she'd seen, like the time she'd woken up to someone choking her, and when she'd opened her eyes, a shadow figure retreated into the mirror. It was enough to make me afraid to look into a mirror in the dark for years. Later on, when all of those ghost hunting shows started to come on, there was an episode about a person who had built a psychomanteum in her closet, this dark room with nothing in it but a chair and a mirror through which she'd channelled spirits. The host of the show gave her an I told you so, reminding her that even if you only invited certain spirits in, you couldn't control which ones crashed the party. The only thing the episode served to do was to make me even more frightened of mirrors in the dark.

The presence in the room was not a physical one. I had no doubt that, besides Belle, I was alone, yet it persisted. There was a brief moment in which I wondered if, by praying to my mom, I hadn't opened up some kind of portal for any old spirit to wander through, but the presence was so peaceful, so serene, so comforting, I realized there was only one explanation for what I was feeling, and that was that my mom had answered my prayers.

"Mom?" I asked the empty room. "Is that you?"

Of course, there was no reply, but the feeling of basking in the presence seemed to grow until the sensation of being enveloped in the love was just this side of overwhelming. It was as if she were saying, "Shhh, mamaleh," which is Yiddish for "little mother". It seems like a weird phrase, but it's a term of affection Jewish parents often use with their little girls.

"Shhh, mamaleh," she seemed to say, "I will protect you. I will watch over you as you sleep. I will always be with you."

It was comforting to know there was someone actually there for me, and me alone, and I fell asleep in the hug of the presence. Whether due to the fact I'd tired myself out crying, or that I knew my mom was out there somewhere, looking out for me, it was one of the best nights' sleeps I've had, either before or since.

CHAPTER TWENTY-SIX

My first impulse the next day was to skip school, camp out in the Food Court, and just wait. Instead, I phoned it in at school so as not to draw any undue attention to myself. When I say I phoned it in, I mean I was there in body, but not in mind or spirit. Each seventy-five minute class passed excruciatingly slow. I watched the hands on the clock move, almost imperceptibly, counting each tick of the red second hand as it made a full lap around the clock's face, watching as the minute hand clicked to the next marker on the perimeter, taking the hour hand with it in an even slower arc.

Lunch was unbearable. I sat with Jem, but all she wanted to do was talk, and my head just wasn't in the game. "Are you mad at me?" she finally said, once she'd grown tired of my grunts in lieu of keeping up my end of the conversation.

"Huh?"

"You're not talking to me," she said, taking a sip of her slushie. The government said they were going to switch to healthier food in the cafeteria. Our school's solution? Fruit juice slushies. All anyone had to do was read the label on a bottle of juice to know there was as much sugar in one of those babies as there was in a can of pop. "Are you okay?"

I looked her in the eyes, and saw tears. For some reason, my moping had really hurt her, and I couldn't figure out why. In that moment, in that split second, I wanted to spill the beans, to tell her everything, and get her to help me sort out this crapstorm I was in. How much could I tell her without giving Jo-Jo away? Without giving Cain away? Without giving myself away?

"Cain's gone," I said.

"Gone?" She put down her slushie. "What do you mean, gone?"

"I mean he left. Jo-Jo went out of town and he went with him."

"Where'd they go? I mean, long-distance relationships aren't ideal, but these days with texting and Skype they're certainly much easier than they used to be. At least, I think they'd *have* to be."

"I don't know."

"He didn't tell you?"

I shook my head. He did say Ottawa, but given the events of the last day, I didn't think he was telling me the truth. He also said it was temporary, just for the protest, but you don't give up your cell number and set your girlfriend up if you plan to come back anytime soon.

"That's rough, Jude."

"Plus all this stuff that's happening downtown..."

"Yeah. That sucks, too."

There was silence between us, but not total silence in the room, because let's face it, we were in the school cafeteria at the time.

"If there's anything I can do to help..."

I shook my head again. Save for turning back the hands of time, there was nothing she could do.

"Well, if you think of something..." She took another sip from her slushie, put it down, and held her hand to her forehead. "Brain freeze," she said.

I couldn't help but smile.

When the afternoon bell rang it was like the fog had lifted. I went directly from school to the mall, made a beeline for the Food Court, and waited. After about ten minutes, I decided I should probably look like I wasn't just hanging for the benefit of the mall cops, so I went to Timmy's, got an Ice Capp and a small box of Timbits, and found a table with a good view of the entire area. I even moved my seat a few times, so the security guards wouldn't notice I'd been there for as long as I was. I had my phone and a battery back-up on hand, in case Cain tried to contact me with a text, rather than in person.

The stores began to close before I knew it, and I decided it was time to go. If he was going to come, I reasoned, he would have done so earlier in the day, during the proverbial rush hour, when school and work let out, before people went home for dinner with their families.

My only family was my dad, Jem, and Cain. Dad was probably still at work, Jem was with her real family, and Cain was laying low with the only family he knew. Dinner was an Ice Capp and three out of six Timbits. I could have taken the last three home with me and stuffed my face with them as I bawled my eyes out before I fell asleep, but decided I'd had enough, and threw them out on my way out of the mall.

The next day at school was pretty much the same as the last, except Jem knew I was mourning over Cain's loss, and that I was, for some reason, horribly affected by the explosion downtown. She wanted me to talk about it, but respected the fact that I just didn't have the words.

No Cain at the mall that night either.

The next day, people started coming forward with stories of their loss connected to the Bay Street Bombing, as it had become known in the media. A boy in grade ten had been absent since the day after, when he'd learned his uncle had been killed, though it wasn't clear if it was his actual uncle, or a close, family friend he called uncle. When I heard, I ran from class to the bathroom to throw up. My teacher could chastise me later for leaving without being excused.

Whether it was his real uncle or not didn't matter—his blood was on my hands.

Rather than give me heck for running out of class, the teacher sent Jem after me. She stood outside of the stall calling my name. "Open up, Jude," she said.

My stomach recoiled and I threw up again, this time only bile, which was good. It meant my stomach had been emptied and might settle soon. Then again, it didn't deserve to settle—Grade Ten Boy's uncle was dead, and it was my fault. I deserved this, and anything else that came with it.

My stomach heaved again. When I was done, I flushed. I left the stall to go to the sink, said, "Go away, Jem," to her as I passed, and went to splash water on my face.

"You don't mean that, Jude. Cain went away. If I go, you'll be alone."

"I don't deserve to have anyone. I'm horrible."

"You're not horrible, you're...tolerable." She said this with a smile, like she was trying to lighten the mood.

"Now *you're* horrible," I told her.

"People move, Jude. Kids move with their parents—"

"He's not a kid—"

"Boys mature slower than girls. Even if he's in his twenties—"

"He's not."

"But even if he was, he'd still be a kid. He probably needs his dad's help, you know, financially. Or maybe his dad needs him."

"He could have given me his number. He could have at least called, or texted, or messaged me, or...something."

"Yes, he could have. The fact that he didn't makes *him* horrible, not you."

But I'd been the one to deliver the package, I wanted to tell her. I was the reason why Grade Ten Boy and so many others were suffering. I was the reason why three people were dead, eight were injured, and a ninth was clinging to his life. I was the reason why the emergency medical service had people scouring the ruins looking for further human remains. I wanted to tell her that I wasn't horrible because Cain had left me, but that I was horrible because I was responsible for all of the death and destruction—that I was the Bay Street Bomber.

I told myself it wasn't me, that I was just the delivery system, that the true perpetrators were Cain and Jo-Jo. Strike that—the true perpetrator was Jo-Jo. I couldn't see Cain going along with something like that. He'd told me he loved me. I didn't see how he could have willingly sent someone he loved to do something as heinous as deliver a bomb to kill innocent people.

Jem smiled. "Are you ready to go back to class? Miss said I should take you to the sick room if you didn't feel up to coming back."

"I can go back to class."

"Are you sure? She said you should go home if you were sick." In my first year at the school there was an epidemic. The Flu had taken our school by storm. People were coming to class sick, making others sick, and it spread like wildfire. People were literally dropping like flies, passing out in the classrooms. Dad had insisted I get a flu shot, so I was okay, but my classes were decimated. It wasn't until after Winter Break that people started coming back and feeling like their normal selves again. I'd been sick in school twice in almost as many days. I imagined the teaching staff had branded me the next Typhoid Mary in their conversations.

"I'm sure," I told her.

CHAPTER TWENTY-SEVEN

That evening was spent in the Food Court again. It was just about eight o'clock and I was ready to give up. I wanted to see Cain, to speak with him, to understand what had happened before I did anything rash, but it seemed as if he wasn't going to show, and I was left to my own devices. I don't know why I was so surprised. I mean, Mom had left me, Dad had left me, Jem would certainly leave me when she found out what I'd done—why shouldn't Cain leave me, too? Wasn't it just a matter of time, anyway?

I knew that if I continued to berate myself like that it was only a matter of time before I started to cry, and a girl crying over her Ice Capp and Timbits was sure to draw someone's attention. Until I'd gotten the whole mess sorted out, attention was the last thing I needed. Lord knows that when the story hit the fan I'd have nothing *but* attention, so I had to lay low for now.

Having eaten my last Timbit, I collected my trash and went to throw it out and head home, and that was when I saw him. At least, I thought it might be him.

There was this guy, standing behind the winding stairway by the movie theatres. He had a thick, dark beard, wore a baseball cap with the bill

174

pulled down low, and dark sunglasses, but there was something about his build, something about the way he leaned against the wall and straightened when we made eye contact, that made me realize it was Cain.

He nodded at me, almost imperceptibly, turned, and walked away.

There was no way I was letting him get away again, so I followed him, keeping no more than ten feet between us. He turned into another alcove and went through double doors marked "Employees Only" without hesitation.

When I reached the doors, I took a quick look around. It was silly, really. I mean, who was to know if I worked in the mall or not? When I was sure no one was watching, I followed him through the doors.

Cain was standing at the end of the corridor, near a fork in the hall. Once the doors had closed behind me, he turned left, and disappeared behind the cinderblock wall.

I practically ran to the end of the hall, took the corner quickly, and almost smacked right into him. He smiled and his dimples rose to the surface, clearly visible, even through his scruff. He'd taken off the sunglasses, and I could see that his eyes were watery.

He took my face in his hands and said, "I've missed you," and then he kissed me. It was gentle at first, but it quickly intensified. At some point, his hat fell off—I remember hearing the soft *plick*, as it hit the concrete floor—but he ignored it. When he broke the kiss, he touched his forehead to mine and said, "I'm so glad it's you."

"Who else would it be?" I said, but not to be confrontational. It just seemed like an odd thing to say. I mean, who else *would* it be?

I guess it could have been the police.

Did he really think I'd sell him out so quickly? That the first thing I'd do was to run to the police?

Wasn't that what any sane person would do?

Any sane person who didn't mind being locked up for the rest of her life.

I guess it would've made sense if I'd have cut a deal with the police.

That entire conversation took place in my head in the space of about a second or two. It ended when Cain said, "I don't know. I'm just glad to see you."

We stood like that, my face cupped in his hands, his forehead next to mind, for a while. But then the conversation in my head started up again, and I had to ask, "What happened, Cain?"

His hands dropped to his sides and he took a step back. "What do you mean?"

"I mean, did you know what was in that last package? Is that why you got that other guy to take me while you disappeared?"

"Jo-Jo said it was time. He thought you were ready."

"What did *you* think, Cain?"

"I agreed."

"You were my boyfriend, Cain. You were supposed to do what's best for me, even if it meant going against Jo-Jo."

"He's my father. I can't go against him."

"You didn't seem to have a problem asking me to go against my father."

"That's different," he said, quite loudly. A door slammed and wheels squeaked somewhere back at the mall end of the corridor. We took a step away from each other and waited in silence until a boy wearing a store uniform pushed a large garbage bin on wheels past us, and disappeared through another set of double doors at the end of the hall.

"That's different," Cain said in a lower voice. "Jo-Jo's not my blood."

"You said he practically adopted you—he can't just throw you back because you oppose him."

Cain shook his head. "Look, it's complicated."

"Uncomplicate it for me."

He exhaled a huge breath of air. "He's more of a father *figure* than a father."

I shrugged. "What's the difference?"

"There's plenty of difference." He looked at me as if he wanted to say more, but either couldn't, or wasn't able to. "He's more of my mentor. He's mentor to all of the kids you saw at his house."

I waited for him to say more. When he didn't, I said, "I'm listening."

"It's complicated, Jude—"

"You've already said that."

He frowned, put his hands on my shoulders, and said, "I was wrong to get you involved like this."

"It's too late for that, Cain," I said coldly. "I'm already involved."

Cain looked off to the side. When he spoke again, it was without eye contact. "Jo-Jo's like my...spiritual leader—"

"What? Like a rabbi? A priest?"

He looked at the ground between us and said, "Jo-Jo's my..." He paused. When he continued, it was like a great exhalation of words and air jumbled together. "Spiritual father. He guides me on my journey on Earth to cleanse my soul so I can continue my journey when I shed my physical body and transcend to heaven." He looked up at me without changing the angle of his head, like he was peering up at me from beneath his brow ridges.

"I'm sorry...what?"

"It sounds crazy, I know, but that's only if you listen with a closed mindset." He took hold of my arms at the biceps, looked me straight in the eyes and continued, "But if you affect an open mindset, you'll see it's not so far from what any other religion preaches." He sounded excited when he spoke. His eyes shone as if with reverence.

"So," I said. I crossed my arms over my chest making it awkward for him to continue holding me like that any longer. "You're in a cult." I'd put two and two together, and came up with five. This conversation made about as much sense as that statement did.

"It's not a cult," he said.

"Then what is it, Cain?"

Cain just looked at me and shook his head, at a loss for words.

"You can't really believe that stuff? That you'll shed your physical body? People who talk that way eventually drink the Kool-Aid when the mothership's in orbit."

"It's not like that—" he said, a bit louder than before.

"Then what *is* it like? Help me understand what it *is* like, Cain."

"Look, Jude: Jo-Jo took me in when I had nowhere else to go. He fed me, clothed me, put a roof over my head, gave me a job...if that's what he believes, then who am I to question it? If he's delusional and this is part of his sickness, then I have his back, same as he has mine."

"But the things you do—"

"Help people," he said, finishing my sentence. "Look at all the people we fed when we raided the dumpster, all the kids that are off the street because Joj takes them in—"

"All the kids whose parents worked on Bay Street who won't be coming home anymore—"

"That was unfortunate. No one was supposed to get hurt. It had a hair-trigger. Someone must've jostled it too much and it went off."

"Think about what you're saying, Cain. *I* jostled it. On the subway. What if it had went off in the subway?"

"Someone must've dropped it, or tried to open the package for it to have gone off like that when it did."

A chill ran down my spine and I shuddered. I thought about Jem and I opening that envelope the other day. If she would have waited until *this* package to get suspicious...

"And you call that good?"

The doors behind us swished and a kid—he was seventeen at best—wearing a mall security uniform nodded as he passed us. We waited until we heard the double doors close at the mall entrance to continue our conversation. It was actually shaping up to be more like an interrogation, but I needed to figure out what was going on.

Was Cain really involved in a cult?

The whole time I thought he was recruiting for a job, was he really recruiting for members?

"Jo-Jo chose that building because it's the perfect storm of corporate corruption.

"There's a designer accounting firm on the top floor who counts some of the higher-ups in the world of hydro among its clientele. Did you know that power costs have more than doubled since this government took over? Did you know there are people who have to choose between feeding their kids and keeping the electricity on? Here—in Ontario."

"That's crappy, but it still doesn't justify—"

"One of the big pharma companies, one of the top suppliers of chemotherapy drugs, has an office on the second floor. That company was involved in a recent scandal where it turns out they were selling watered-down chemo drugs to hospitals to save on production costs. People died because they were only getting a fraction of the meds they needed to beat the disease—"

"That sounds like a job for the police to me."

"It's under investigation, but if we're talking body count..."

"You're not God, you know! It's not up to you to decide how or if people atone for their sins." Cain opened his mouth as if to speak, but I cut him off, saying, "And neither's Jo-Jo."

He said nothing for a moment, but he looked hurt enough to cry. When it became clear he wasn't going to speak, I continued. "I don't understand," I said. "If you have something to say, why not take to social media or something?"

"Like in peaceful protests?" He chuckled. "You've read the news, Jude. Peaceful protests are here today, gone tomorrow. To initiate any sort of lasting change you have to go big or go home. Black Lives Matter made it into the news because of their less than conventional behaviour during the protest and was forgotten a few days later.

"People gathered at Queen's Park to protest for the de-criminalization of marijuana. News coverage for that faded pretty much the day after the protest ended.

"The protest against Islamophobia was all over the news for about 48 hours, at most—"

"What about the occupy movement? Idle No More? The G-20 protests? Those are still in the news today, years later. *They* were peaceful—"

"Until they weren't anymore. People were killed at Idle No More, and brutalized by the police at G-20 and Occupy Toronto. It's because they turned violent that they had staying power. *That's* how you make social change, by shocking the public out of their safety bubbles."

"So run through the downtown core naked, spray paint something that says something that matters in a place that matters—" I was gesticulating with my arms, tears were rolling down my cheeks. How did I get myself into this mess? How could my trust have been so misplaced? Cain was like the modern-day embodiment of the Trojan horse—he was the most attractive person I'd ever seen in person, but he hid a deep, dark, destructive secret. Only instead of ending a decades-long war, he essentially ended my life with his subterfuge.

Cain grabbed my arms at the wrists and held them. My hands formed tight fists between us. "The bottom line is that whether or not I believe Jo-Jo's religious dogma, whether or not I subscribe to his philosophy of the afterlife, he's trying to effect social change. Bottom line? He's doing good."

I pulled my arms from his grasp, crossed them in front of my chest once more, and said, "Funny. I never thought of good as being subjective."

We stared at each other for a moment or two and I said, "So now what?" breaking the silence.

"I need to disappear, Jude. Jo-Jo doesn't even know I'm here. If he did—"

"What? He'd kill you?"

Cain shrugged and shook his head, as if to say he didn't know what Jo-Jo was capable of.

"Not seriously?"

He shrugged his shoulders again. "People don't leave the organization once they join, Jude."

Something about that statement, the finality of it, the way he'd said it, made me feel sorry for him, like he was in over his head, like he felt indebted to Jo-Jo and wanted out but didn't know how. I rushed him in an embrace and held him tightly. "We can go to the police together," I said. "If we turn him in, maybe they'll go easy on us."

Cain pushed me away, but held me at arm's length. "I can't turn him in, Jude. I owe him."

"*I* don't."

"He gave you a job when no one else would."

"Big deal. It was a job, nothing else."

"You took his money, Jude. It was blood money."

"That only counts if I knew."

There was another pause during which he let go of me. "The way I see it, you have two choices: you could come with me, or you could turn us in. If you turn us in, you'll wind up taking the blame. They'll never find us because we essentially live off the grid, and before long they'll start to think you made us up to deflect the blame. They'll start looking at you for the bombing.

"If you come with us—"

"If I go with you, I'm accepting that what I did was okay, that my life, my *freedom*, is more important than the lives of those other people, the ones we've already killed and any others that might die in the future."

"It's for the greater good, Jude."

"Says who?"

"Says Jo-Jo. Our souls can only be cleansed in a river of blood—"

"That from his manifesto?"

"Something like that."

"And that's what you believe?"

He reached for me and pulled me close, stroking the back of my head. "The question is: do *you* believe?"

"And if I don't?"

"That's something only you can decide."

He stopped stroking and used the hand to pull me even closer to him. "Forty-eight hours, that's all I can give you. You need to choose: me, or your life in the wake of the bombing. You can turn yourself in if you think that's the right thing to do, or you can come with us and change the world for the better, choose to make the world *right*," he whispered into my ear.

Cain took a step away from me and cupped my face in his hands again; our meeting had come full circle. "Forty-eight hours, Jude." He touched his lips to mine in something just short of a kiss. "I'll find you," he said, and then he turned and left.

I watched as he disappeared further into the service halls forming the bowels of the mall, unsure of whether I loved him or hated him more.

CHAPTER TWENTY-EIGHT

And that's my story."

"Who knows you're here."

"No one. I saw you on a commercial and came straight over."

"There's no address on the commercial."

"So, I looked you up online first, but then I came straight over."

"No one knows? Not your dad, or your friend with the cartoon name, or your boyfriend?"

"Her name's Jem, and no."

"Give me five dollars."

I look at her through the squinted eyes of distrust. "Your commercial said the consultation was free."

"Yeah, for traffic citations, or trespassing or...shoplifting. But you're talking about terrorism here, with a capital T."

I'm still looking at her as if I'm trying to figure out if she's for real.

"You got any money on you, kid?"

After a belly-deep sigh, I open my purse, pull a five from my wallet, and toss it onto her desk. It's so light, it's like a feather wafting in the breeze and I think of how I'd look like a dufus if I had to get up to pick it up from the ground.

It eventually settles in front of her on the desk after skimming the surface a bit. It reminds me of the time Cain and I went to the waterfront and tried skipping stones from the outcropping on the beach.

"Consider this my retainer," she says. "It cements our lawyer-client confidentiality pact.

"As your lawyer," she continues, "I suggest we go to the police together, insist we speak with the Crown Attorney and try to cut a deal."

"Give myself up?"

She nods, leans forward in her chair, and rests her elbows on the desk, her chin on steepled fingers.

"I thought you were on my side."

"I'm on the side of the law." She smiles, chuckles, then sinks back into her chair. "As corny as that sounds."

"Why would you suggest I give myself up, then?"

"You were duped. Your 'boyfriend'," and I swear she says it just like that, with air-quotes that are almost audible, "is no different than those guys who target older women and take them for all they're worth."

When I say nothing she continues, "In other words, he's a con-artist."

That's absurd. Cain loves me. He said so. I want to tell her this, but she must read it on my face, because she says, "Told you he loved you, did he?" in a mocking sort of tone that makes me want to slap her smirk right off her face.

"Let's cut to the chase, here. Your boyfriend belongs to a cult. That Jo-Jo guy is the leader. He's been recruiting you."

There's that word again—recruit. I remember the ad I was told to place to get Cain's attention: Recruits Wanted.

No. He's a recruiter because he recruits people to make Jo-Jo's deliveries. He's a head-hunter-type recruiter, nothing more.

"A young girl, an essential loner with mommy and daddy issues—the perfect prey."

"I'm not—"

I stop because she's right. I am a loner. Aside from Jem, I have no friends. My mom is dead and rotting in her grave, and my dad might as well be for the amount of time we've spent together since her death. I've known for a long time that when my mom died I lost both of my parents. I've just been too much in denial to ever vocalize it.

"Jo-Jo and his gang are nothing more than a bunch of eco-terrorists who corrupt innocent, young, disenfranchised kids, mostly girls, and get them to do their dirty work for them."

The faces of the Home Wrecker Girls flash through my mind. Cain's explanation that he'd dated one of them.

No! I refuse to believe it.

Cain *loves* me. He gave me 48 hours. Forty-eight hours and then he's going to come and get me and we can be together.

"If we give them up, Cain and this...Jo-Jo guy, we can ask the Crown for immunity. You'll be branded a hero instead of a patsy once this hits the press."

"Cain's not a terrorist," I say. I mean for it to sound brave. Instead, it sounds nothing short of feeble.

"Get your head out of the aughts," she says to me. "Terrorists come in all shapes and sizes these days, foreign and homegrown, given what's been happening in North America lately.

"Eco-terrorists go after the big corporations they believe are killing the world. They do stuff to expose them, like sabotage an oil rig to show how easy it is to spoil the environment with an oil spill—"

"I know what eco-terrorism is, I'm not stupid."

"Really? 'Cause the story you just told me would seem to contradict that assertion."

"He's not a terrorist, eco or any other kind. He just wants to make the world a better place."

"By bombing the hell out of it? Look, kid, at this point, no one knows of your involvement but me and Cain's guys—"

"Jo-Jo's guys."

"Whatever. My point is: you have a choice to make. Either you come clean to the authorities, or you go with your boyfriend and hope no one figures out it was you."

"But it wasn't me. You don't even know it was Jo-Jo."

She smirks, and says, "If not him, then whom?"

"Maybe that John guy acted alone."

"No way the authorities like that." She leans forward in her chair again, her forearms on the desk. "I tell you what they *are* going to like: you. For three murders, assault with intent to do bodily harm on at least nine others, illegal firearms, terrorism, treason...should I go on?"

Speechless, all I can do is shake my head.

"You're sixteen, old enough to be tried as an adult. If convicted, there won't be word one mentioned about juvy—you'll go to prison, full out."

"If I could save Cain? Say he's an innocent in all of this, too."

"Cut off the snake at the head? I doubt Cain would come out clean.

"You realize that if I'm your lawyer I can't be his, too. Cain's lawyer would argue you were fully aware of what was going on, that you willingly and with malice aforethought planted that bomb. He has plausible deniability in that he didn't give you the box; this guy, John, did."

"Cain wouldn't do that to me."

She purses her lips, like duck-lips in a selfie, and says, "That's sweet. After everything I've told you, you still think he loves you.

"Snap out of it, kid. Did you hear what I just said? You're old enough to be tried as an adult. It's time to start acting like one."

"I don't know. It's a lot to take in at once."

"Tic-tock, kid. Your boyfriend gave you 48 hours yesterday evening. Clock's ticking. By my calculations, you have just over half that left. Not much time for the authorities to mount a sting."

"I need some time to think."

"I get 90 dollars per hour. You gave me five. The way I see it, your retainer's already run out. I'll give you 12 hours, till start of business day tomorrow. If you want to do the right thing, I'll be here waiting for you."

"And if I don't?"

"You *don't* want to do the right thing?"

"If I think the right thing is going with Cain?"

She shook her head and narrowed her eyes at me. "You think the right thing is joining a cult of eco-terrorists?"

My first impulse is to defend Cain. To say he's not in a cult and that he's not an eco-terrorist, but she'd only have another comeback, and time was wasting. I was on the clock. I needed to go home and think.

"If you think the right thing is joining a cult of eco-terrorists, then *gai gezunterhait*:

I know that phrase: *gai gezunterhait*. It's Yiddish for go in good health.

CHAPTER TWENTY-NINE

T hough I refuse to believe the lawyer was right about Jo-Jo, and certainly not about Cain, she *was* right about one thing: I had a decision to make.

I could stay here in this stupid, do nothing, all alone life, or run away with Cain.

Well, when you put it that way...

I couldn't just leave without thinking of my dad, who was sitting on the couch watching *Judge Judy* reruns when I got home.

"Hey, kiddo," he says when I walk in. He sits straight up on the edge of the couch. "Where have you been? I was getting worried."

"I went for a walk."

"That's not like you." He turns the television off. "Is everything okay?"

I shake my head and the tears start to flow, like, uncontrollably, because I feel bad for the guy. I mean, his daughter's either going to leave or go to jail for a very long time. And though the lawyer said she could *probably* get amnesty for me if I turned Cain in, probably's like an oxymoron all unto itself. It implies a small measure of doubt, but sometimes, a small measure of doubt is huge, because it's all that's standing between life and death.

"Hey, hey, hey," he says, getting up from his seat. "Come talk to me." He puts an arm around my shoulder, seems to produce a box of Kleenex from nowhere, like those grannies who abracadabra a tissue from their sleeves, and says, "What's going on?"

It's a turning point. Now's my chance to come clean, to unburden my soul, to tell him everything, and to dash his hopes and dreams about his little girl's future, now and forever.

"Cain broke up with me," I bawl, barely intelligible, to myself, anyway, between the sobs.

"Oh, honey," he says. "I'm sorry, but you'll find there will be many boys in your life, some will break your heart, some whose heart you'll break."

"But I loved him, Dad, I mean, really loved him, like I could see us spending the rest of our lives together loved him—"

"You're only sixteen, Jude. This isn't my parents' era when people get married right after high school. You have your whole life ahead of you: school, a career, and as much as I hate to admit it, more boys."

"He said he loved me."

His next words are spoken in a grave tone, much more serious than the encouraging tone of his earlier statement. "You're not pregnant, are you?"

"Dad!"

"I need to ask, Jude. I mean, I'm just trying to gauge the situation here and—"

"Cain and I never—"

"Good, because since we're talking, I need you to promise me that when the time comes you'll use protection. And I don't mean condoms—"

This is *not* how I saw the conversation going. He really doesn't get it, does he?

Most adults would claim I'm the one that doesn't get it at this point. Dad's putting himself out there, doing an awkward thing, talking to his daughter about sex. The thing is, I do. Get it, I mean. But the issue at hand is so much deeper than the fact that Cain and I never...you know.

"I'm not having this conversation with you," I say.

"And we don't have to have this conversation if you promise me you'll see your doctor for protection when the time comes. Now, I don't have to go with you. You have a good head on your shoulders and I trust you—"

If he only knew.

"Okay! Okay. I promise. Now, can we just change the subject?"

He shifts a pillow on the couch and sinks back into it.

"What happened? With Cain, I mean."

"He's moving away."

"Where to?"

"He won't tell me."

"Ouch!" he says. He really does look pained, as if my pain is his or something. "That's rough."

My sobs have long subsided into sniffles, but there's still a fairly steady stream of tears down my cheeks. Dad hands me the Kleenex box again.

"Look, Jude, I don't want to give you platitudes, here, but there are so many more fish in the sea."

I know Dad loves me and all, but if the best material he has is there are more fish in the sea?

I do a mental T-chart of Dad versus Cain.

In the Dad column, I have:

He loves me unconditionally.

He would never up and leave.

He's at work more than he's here.

He doesn't know what to say to me to make me feel special.

He offers me security as best as he can with the house, and the fridge and pantry are always full, and with good food, too.

The bills are always paid.

All I have to do is concentrate on school, which is boring, but he's planning for my future.

Now, for the Cain column:

He loves me—maybe not unconditionally, but with an intensity Dad could never match.

He upped and left, but he came back, and now he wants me to leave with him.

He's always there for me; he's never missed responding to one of my texts, or the newspaper ad.

He knows exactly what to say (and do) to make me feel special.

He offered me security by giving me a job when no one else would, Jo-Jo's house was always open to me, and though the food was cheap and not exactly healthy, at least it was there.

Delivering packages for Jo-Jo would have paid the bills, eventually.

I'd have to leave school, but we'd be doing good things for the future of the world, feeding the homeless, clearing pollution...and bombing innocents to prove a point—

Enough! I don't just mentally erase the T-chart, I crumple it up and set it on fire before tossing it in the trash and watching it burn.

When I tune back in, Dad's still going on about how I'm still young, and Cain was just the first of many, and that I'm entitled to mourn the loss of whatever I thought I might have with him in the future, and how every day it will get a little better.

"How many more days before it gets better with Mom?"

His face drops, like, literally drops, as if his skin's about to slide from his skull and into his lap, and I realize I couldn't have hurt him more if I'd slapped him. I don't think that was my original intention, to hurt him like that, but Mom's been dead for years, and I'm still not over the loss. If I'm busy mourning over the loss of Cain, how can I even think about the other fish? And do I really want to start?

"That's not the same, Judith."

The room grows noticeably cold. He went from honey to Jude to Judith in minutes flat.

"I think it is."

He slides a bit forward in his seat and twists his body so he's facing me. "Your mother is dead. There's no coming back from death."

"So you're saying that Cain and I might get back together."

"No, that is not what I'm saying."

"Then he's gone from my life forever, just like Mom is."

"No," he says. He's sitting on the edge of the pillow now, balanced precariously—if the pillow slides forward even an inch, he'll slide right onto the carpet. "That's not what I'm saying."

"Then what, exactly, are you saying?"

"Are you deliberately trying to get my goat?" he asks. "I get it: you're miserable and you want everyone around you to be miserable."

"You're doing fine on that front all by yourself," I say, almost before I know I'm going to say it. How did this happen? How did my need for my father's comfort turn into all out war?

Maybe he's right. Maybe if he sees how horrible a person I really am, if he hates me as much as I hate myself, the news of what happened might not be as painful.

"Judith? I love you, and I want you to be happy. But right now you are pushing some pretty powerful buttons and I can't continue this conversation any longer. If you want to sit here with me and watch television, maybe order a pizza, you're welcome, but if you insist on pushing my buttons, you need to go to your room."

For some reason I can't resist rubbing salt into the wound. "Aren't I a little old for being sent to my room?"

"Go to your room," he says, calmer than I might be able to manage if our positions were reversed. "Now!"

I just stand there, contemplating my next move.

"One," he says, counting. It was something he used to do when I was a kid. If I did what he wanted on zero, I was good. One was okay because he acknowledged I needed some time to think. Two was still okay because I needed a bit more time to consider the situation. God forbid I waited until three.

"This is stupid."

"Two," he says, a bit more sternly than before.

"What happens when you get to three?"

"You don't want to know."

"I'm not a child anymore, you know," I say, and stomp up the stairs.

"Your behaviour right now would seem to contradict that statement," he calls after me.

The way the walls shake, the noise the door makes when I slam it, is somehow incredibly satisfying.

CHAPTER THIRTY

I *need help*, I text Jem, but delete it before I press send.

I'm in trouble, I type, but delete that as well because she might think I'm telling her I'm pregnant.

Cain contacted me. I delete that, too. If Cain's on the run, the last thing I want to do is have to give him up. And though I could send the message and then delete it, according to the stuff you see on television, it's only deleted from my phone but not from the server, and the police can still access it.

I call her number up on my contacts list instead. My thumb hovers over the green receiver icon before I make the call. Doesn't National Security have software that listens in on phone calls for key words? So, okay, the NSA probably has no jurisdiction in Canada, but what if CSIS was doing the same thing? We share the longest, undefended border in the world; is it such a stretch to think we'd share software, too?

What would I tell her anyway? Hey, Jem, you were right: Jo-Jo's up to no good. He booby-trapped a package, people died, the police are probably looking for me (not to mention CSIS with the help of the NSA), and a lawyer told me to turn myself in. Not to mention the fact that I just broke my dad's heart.

Oh, and did I mention that I'm thinking of running away with Cain? Nothing like tearing your dad's broken but still beating heart out of his chest and stomping on it for good measure.

Meet me in the park in 10? I type. This time I do press send.

Jem replies seconds later: *Kk*

My room overlooks the peak of the garage roof at the front of the house. Dad and I had always discussed how this would be the ideal escape route in case of a fire. All I had to do was to open the window, kick out the screen, climb onto the roof, slide down to the eaves trough until I was hanging off of it, and jump.

"Oh, is that all?" I remember asking Dad.

Dad was still watching television quite loudly in the front room where he had a great view of the stairs, main hall, and front door. Given that Dad's trying to drown out his thoughts with the volume, he might not hear the creak of my feet on the stairs as I descend, but the front door's in his full, unobstructed view, and the sliding door in the back sticks, so there's no way I'm escaping from ground level.

Time to put Dad's fire route escape plan to the test.

Rather than kick out the screen, I remove it and bring it back into my room. The last thing I need is for him to hear the screen as it clatters down the garage roof and lands on the ground outside the house. If it lands on the grassy side, between houses, I might be safe. But if it lands on the other side at the front of the house, he might hear it when it clanks against the front walk.

Shimmying out of the window is more difficult than I'd thought. A while ago we'd replaced the large sliding windows with smaller crank ones, a fact Dad had never figured into his escape plan. It was hard enough for me to squeeze myself through the opening, and I wonder how Dad, with his broad shoulders and football physique (as Mom used to call it) would ever manage.

There's a brief moment when I realize there's only one way back into the house, but I push that out of my mind. Whatever punishment Dad gives me pales in comparison to whatever the courts will assign. The thought is oddly empowering. Even the height, the slide down the roof, and the jump is nothing by comparison. What was a scrape, or sprained or broken limb when stacked up against life in prison?

I'm already on a swing when Jem arrives at the park. I'm sitting in the very same swing as when Cain and I had professed our mutual love, not too long ago. Jem smiles at me and then, ironically, takes the same swing Cain used on that very day, only rather than face each other, we both face the same way. Our feet are planted in the woodchips beneath us as we rock ourselves forward and back, almost in unison.

"You okay?" Jem asks after a while.

At first I don't answer, but then I start to shake my head and tear up. Before I know it I'm sobbing openly.

"Fudge, Jude, what happened? Is this still about Cain leaving?"

I decide to ignore the "still" in her comment because she's never had a boyfriend and she wouldn't know the heartache I feel.

Then I remind myself that Cain's not gone, not yet, and that I can still go with him if I choose.

I'm still shaking my head as I bury it in my hands.

"Hey, Jude...tell me what's going on. Is it your dad?"

I draw my hands down my face and take a deep breath through my nose as I do. It sounds like a snort, and I sort of want to laugh, but I don't because a huge sob takes me over instead. My hands pause over my mouth and then fall to my lap. "He's not talking to me." I chance a glance up at her. "My dad, I mean, not Cain."

Jem gasps. "You've heard from Cain?"

Wait...how did she know that? Is that what they call a Freudian slip, letting her know of what I was thinking without actually knowing I was saying it?

I look away from her and nod again.

"What did he say?"

I shrug. "I'm in trouble, Jem, like, deep trouble."

"Are you—"

Told you so. "No! I'm not *pregnant*." Being pregnant would almost be a blessing by comparison to the trouble I'm in.

"Oh."

"You sound disappointed."

"I'm not, I just...you're freaking me out, Jude. What happened?"

Time to rip the Band-Aid off, I guess. "I did something bad, but I didn't know it was bad at the time—"

"What was it?"

"I'm not going to tell you."

"Oh," she says. Her posture slumps and her shoulders round in an exaggerated show of disappointment.

"Don't be like that. This is serious stuff and I don't want to implicate you. It's what they call plausible deniability."

She pauses for a beat and then says, "Go on."

"Cain's involved. That's why he's leaving. He's asked me to go with him."

Jem twists her swing around until she's facing me. "You're not seriously—"

"No! No. At least, I don't think so."

"You can't go with him. You'll leave your dad alone. You'll break his heart."

"I think I already have."

She squints at me and tilts her head a bit as if she doesn't understand.

"I said some really stupid things to him before I left. I had to sneak out to come meet you."

"You snuck out?"

"Through my bedroom window."

"You really are bad ass!"

You ain't heard nothin' yet, I want to tell her. If sneaking out of my room impresses her...

"I'm not. I'm just plain bad. I'm a horrible person." I hang my head and close my eyes. They've already begun to burn with tears of shame.

"You're not horrible," she says, sort of soothingly. "You're just confused."

I'm not confused, I want to say, I'm thinking of going with him and I need you to talk me out of it, but all I can do is shake my head and sob openly, unable to get any words out.

"Your dad will forgive you, you know."

For being a murderer? A terrorist? I don't think so. The words form in my head but my heavy breathing prevents them from coming out through my mouth.

"He just needs some time."

I take a deep, belly breath like they tell us to do in Fitness at school and manage, "He won't. Besides, I *don't* have time. Cain gave me 48 hours, and that was, like, 40 hours ago, so..."

"You're seriously thinking of leaving with him?"

I nod.

"But your dad?"

"My father'll probably be glad I'm not his burden anymore. I mean, think of it, Jem—I'm practically seventeen. I can move out on my own when I'm eighteen and I don't even have to tell him where I am if I don't want to. The police won't care if I'm gone a little early." Not until they figure out I'm the bomber, that is.

"You'll be leaving him alone—"

"Oh, you mean like he always leaves me alone?"

"Where's all this anger coming from? I thought you and your dad were copacetic."

She's right. We *were* okay. We were always okay. I wrack my brain trying to remember the point at which we were no longer okay, and though I know the answer, I refuse to believe Cain is the reason. It was bound to happen sooner or later, I reason, my finding a boyfriend, my growing up.

"We were," I say, "and now we're not."

"Fine. Never mind your dad. What about me?"

"What about you?" I ask.

"Gee, Jude, thanks." She starts to get up, as if to leave, but I grab her arm and pull her back.

"I mean, there's no reason why *we* can't keep in touch."

Jem's arm relaxes in my grip and she sits back down.

"So long as you don't spill the beans about my location to my dad."

"I don't know, Jude..."

We look at each other and then Jem says, "You said you had eight hours to think about it, just...promise me you'll take the full eight hours and that you won't do anything rash. Promise me that when you go back home you won't aggravate your father further."

When I don't say anything she repeats, "Promise me."

"I promise."

CHAPTER THIRTY-ONE

We keep a spare key in the garage, so I was able to let myself in without ringing or knocking. Best case scenario? Dad respected my privacy (read: he was so disgusted with me) he didn't even try to patch things up with me before going to bed. Worst case? He tried to patch things up, went into my room, discovered I was gone, and is waiting up for me.

Turns out it was the medium case scenario: he'd fallen asleep on the couch, the TV still blaring. I let myself in, close the front door as quietly as I can, and slide the dead-bolt into place as slowly as humanly possible. Unfortunately, the click isn't quiet enough and it wakes him.

It could have been worse. He could have put the safety bolt on and the alarm in which case I'd have no choice but to ring the bell to get back in.

He must think I've just come down the stairs because he says, "Look, honey, I've been thinking." He turns to face me and pats the seat cushion beside him. "I know you're still young. I also know that losing your mom was a huge trauma."

"Dad—" I start, but whether it's to stop him or spill the beans about my situation, I don't know yet.

"Now, I know that if your mother was still here she'd know exactly what to say. I'm kind of at a loss because I was never a teenage girl, but I can imagine that breaking off with your first boyfriend can feel like he's ripped your heart into tiny little pieces.

"I flew off the handle earlier, and I'm sorry. I just miss her so much."

"I do, too," I say and lean into his armpit. He puts his arm around my shoulder and pulls me close, and I try to gauge which hug makes me feel safer: his or Cain's.

Right now it's Dad's, but once I tell him my secret, he'll probably never want to hug me again.

Cain, on the other hand, knows my secret, is in it with me, and still wants to be with me.

Point: Cain.

If Dad knew about my secret, he'd probably march me back to that lawyer's office, and then the two of them would march me to the police department. He'd convince me to give Cain and Jo-Jo up in exchange for my freedom, and pay my legal fees. Though he may never let me out of his sight again—or he may never want to look at me again—he'd most likely be at my side through the ordeal.

Cain wants to run away and pretend as if it never happened. I'd be on the run forever. If I went with Cain, I'd be just as guilty as he and Jo-Jo, just as responsible as them for those people's deaths, too.

Point: Dad.

"Care to share your issue with me?"

Though I shake my head, it barely moves, cradled against Dad's chest the way it is.

"Fair enough. I promise to let it be as long as you promise to tell me what it is when you're ready."

"Mmm," I say.

"Should I take that as a yes?"

He's being so nice to me after I was so horrible to him, and I can't help but wonder if this is what unconditional love feels like.

Cain says he loves me, but if I'm not ready to go with him, he'll just disappear. If you love someone, I mean, truly love someone, shouldn't you want to be with them? Wouldn't leaving them alone forever be the last thing you wanted to do?

Point: Dad.

I blink. A tear falls from my eyes and trickles down my cheek. Dad must feel the wet spot where it soaks into his shirt because he says, "Hey, hey, hey...why the tears?"

Then again, if Cain loves me, maybe leaving me is the best thing he could do for me. Maybe he knows he's in trouble and doesn't want me to be forever on the run. Maybe his leaving is opening the door for me to clear my name and get on with my life.

Point: Cain.

I have to ask myself: if I love my father, shouldn't I want the same for him? Shouldn't I be offering him the opportunity to get on with his life, rather than being bogged down with further misery, having to watch me be arrested and vilified in the media as the Bay Street Bomber?

Another point: Cain.

"Why are you crying, kiddo?" Dad asks again.

"Tears of joy," I tell him. "I love you, Dad," I say, leaning over to kiss him on the cheek.

Dad and I watch a PVR'd show or two and then I say goodnight and go back up to my room. And while one disaster has been averted—Dad never knew I'd left the house—another huge disaster of earth-shattering proportions still looms. Eventually, they're going to find something to tie me back to the explosion: a snippet of video, a fingerprint (no one suggested I wear gloves), a hair...

I think my tantrum from earlier in the evening is all my dad could bear for a single day. I've noticed that, since we lost Mom, even the smallest of things set him off, like he's teetering on the edge of a precipice, and it doesn't take much to send his sanity over the edge.

Trouble is, I don't have another day to spare. My 48-hour deadline is looming and I have to make a choice: Cain and Jo-Jo, or Dad and Jem. And while I know that's simplifying things—like *total* understatement—it's what it boils down to, isn't it? Choose Cain and Jo-Jo or choose Dad and Jem.

Choose Cain and Jo-Jo and I'm happy. I may even be able to evade prosecution.

Choose Dad and Jem, face certain prosecution, and lose one or possibly both of them.

Though it seems like anything but, due to a process of elimination, the solution is simple.

Dad's been through enough. He's still reeling from Mom's loss. He might never recover after losing me, too, but at least he'll know I'm still alive. To be sure, I leave him a note:

Dad,

Cain's leaving and I'm going with him. Don't try to follow me. It's better this way, you'll see...

And he will. See, I mean. Eventually.

If I can, I'll check in with you. I know what you're thinking, that this is some kind of selfish move. Maybe one day you'll see that this is the most selfless thing I can do, although I pray you don't, and that's part of the reason why I have to leave.

Please don't try to find me as it will only make the matter worse.

It occurs to me as I'm writing that no parent in his right mind would ever accept that, and knowing Dad, he'll probably search for me for the rest of his life. I'm counting on what I said above, about his sanity being on a precipice, that he won't have the energy to come after me.

I love you,

Jude

When I'm done, I return to the comfort of my bed, one last time.

Confession time: though most of what I told the lawyer was true, there was one thing I left out. When Cain and I parted ways back at the mall, he didn't tell me he'd find me over the next 48 hours. He told me to call him over the next 48 hours, when I was ready to leave.

He handed me a pre-paid cell phone.

There was one number programmed into it.

I press the number and press send.

ABOUT THE AUTHOR

Elise Abram is high school teacher of English and Computer Studies, former archaeologist, editor, publisher, award winning author, avid reader of literary and science fiction, and student of the human condition. Everything she does, watches, reads and hears is fodder for her writing. She is passionate about her morning lattes, writing and language, cooking, differentiated instruction, and ABC's *Once Upon A Time*. In her spare time, she experiments with paleo cookery, knits badly, and writes. She also bakes. Most of the time it doesn't burn. Her family doesn't seem to mind.

http://eliseabram.com

bed, is found by police, and taken home to meet her four-year-old self that she realizes she's been time travelling.

Alice is unsure if her getting unstuck in time should be considered an ability or a liability, until she disappears right in front of her high school at dismissal time, the busiest time of day. Worried that someone may find out about her problem before long, Alice enlists her best friend (and maybe boyfriend), Pete, to help her try to control her shifting through time with limited success. She's just about ready to give up when the shooter is caught. Alice resolves to take control of her time travelling in order to go back to That Day, stop the shooting, and figure out the identity of the stranger who'd shielded Alice's body with her own.

ALSO BY ELISE ABRAM

THE REVENANT

A YA PARANORMAL THRILLER WITH ZOMBIES!

Raised from the dead as a revenant more than a hundred years ago, Zulu possesses Spiderman's stealth, Superman's speed, and Batman's keen intellect. His only companion is Morgan the Seer, an old man cursed with longevity and the ability to see the future in his dreams. Zulu has spent the last century training with Morgan in order to save the people in his nightmares from certain and violent death. Branded a vigilante by the Media, Zulu must live his life in the shadows, travelling by night or in the city's underground unless his quest demands otherwise.

Kat is an empath, someone who sees emotions as colourful auras. Relentlessly bullied by her peers, and believing her life amounts to nothing but a huge cosmic mistake, she finds purpose in her abilities when she is recruited to help Zulu and Morgan complete their missions.

Malchus is Morgan's long dead twin brother. A powerful necromancer, Malchus manages to find a way to return to the living, and he has a score to settle with Morgan. Believing Morgan responsible for his death and out to seek revenge, Malchus begins to raise an army of undead minions and use them to hunt Morgan down. As Malchus closes in on Morgan and his charges, the trio soon realizes the people most in need of saving are themselves.

IF YOU LIKED *PHASE SHIFT*

YOU WON'T WANT TO MISS

MOLLY AND PALMER IN

THROWAWAY CHILD

The skeleton of a young girl is found beneath the cement basement floor in an abandoned Victorian in Toronto. On duty is Detective Constable Michael Crestwood who contacts forensic anthropologist Dr. Palmer Richardson to assist in the investigation. What they uncover is the story of a six year old Cree girl, stolen from her family, warehoused in a government run facility and then forgotten.

In a story with ties to current headlines, THROWAWAY CHILD explores the injustice experienced by two girls imprisoned in a mid-twentieth century residential school and the tragic fallout ensuing as a result of one girl's need to find a home.

IF YOU ENJOYED

PHASE SHIFT AND *THROWAWAY CHILD,*

YOU HAVE TO READ

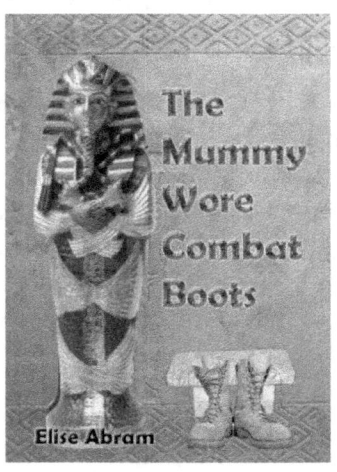

When called to investigate an uncatalogued sarcophagus found in storage at the Royal Ontario Museum, forensic anthropologist Palmer Richardson has his work cut out for him. When the mummy inside proves to be that of a teenage boy, Palmer joins Detective Constable Michael Crestwood of the Metropolitan Toronto Police. in an investigation delving into the world of online gaming where losing health points in a skirmish could have serious implications for a player's life in the real world.

Inspired by real-life headlines, THE MUMMY WORE COMBAT BOOTS highlights the growing divide between children who live their lives immersed in a digital culture and the adults tasked with raising them who live in the real world.